MESSY PERFECT LOVE

THE JETTY BEACH SERIES BOOK 3

CLAIRE KINGSLEY

Always Have LLC

Copyright © 2016 Claire Kingsley

All rights reserved.

No part of this book may be reproduced in any form or by any electronic or mechanical means, including information storage and retrieval systems, without written permission from the author, except for the use of brief quotations in a book review.

This is a work of fiction. Any names, characters, places, or incidents are products of the author's imagination and used in a fictitious manner. Any resemblance to actual people, places, or events is purely coincidental or fictionalized.

Edited by Larks and Katydids

Cover by Kari March Designs

Published by Always Have, LLC

Previously published as Must Be Fate: A Jetty Beach Romance

ISBN: 9781797051550

www.clairekingsleybooks.com

❦ Created with Vellum

ABOUT THIS BOOK

Messy Perfect Love was originally published as Must Be Fate: A Jetty Beach Romance.

When opposites attract, it's messy… and perfect

From the moment Clover crashes into my life, she turns my world upside down. She's quirky and fun—unlike any woman I've ever known.

Her wild ideas pull me out of my comfort zone, and I love the way she makes me feel. But her free spirit longs to roam, and I don't know if she can do the one thing I really need. Stay.

I'm sure fate led me to Jetty Beach, but until I meet Cody Jacobsen, I'm not sure why. The small-town doctor—with his gorgeous body, ridiculous dimples, and adorable bedside manner—sweeps me off my feet and saves the day. Literally.

Our chemistry is off the charts. But to a man like him—mature and put together—I'm a wild breeze who throws him off kilter. And for a woman like me—who never truly lets anyone in—he might want more than I can give.

He might want everything.

1

CLOVER

The line is practically out the door, and I can't make espresso fast enough.

My mass of curly blond hair keeps trying to break free of my hair tie while I work. I blow a curl out of my eye while I steam a pitcher of two percent. That's right, isn't it? The customer wants two percent? Or was that the customer before? Shoot, I can't remember. The café has been slammed for the last hour and my head is spinning.

I finish up the drink and put a lid on the cup. I hate working in a place that uses paper cups, but what are you gonna do? I need to make rent.

"Mark," I call out, reading the name on the cup. "Twelve-ounce double shot vanilla latte."

A man in a button-down shirt and tie comes forward. I flash him my friendliest smile. He looks annoyed.

"Thanks for coming in," I say, my voice cheery.

His face softens as he grabs his coffee, and he gives me a closed-mouth smile. I feel my grin grow larger. He had to wait for his coffee, but I broke through his grumpy exterior. I call that a victory.

I take a deep breath, and go to work on the next drink. One of my coworkers brushes past me and I freeze. I don't want to spill anything. I'm on thin ice with Dean, my boss, already; screwing up in the middle of a rush will probably get me fired.

I cannot afford to get fired.

"Clover, can you work the register for a second?" Dean asks as he walks by me.

I run the back of my arm over my forehead and nod. "Sure." My feet are killing me, but my shift is almost over. I just have to get through this line, and I can go home.

"What can I get for you?" I ask the next customer in line.

"Are you guys short-staffed or something?" he asks.

"Oh, you know, unexpected rush. Sorry for the wait. We'll make sure the coffee is worth it."

He orders his drink and I write it down on the side of the cup. I break out my smile again for the next customer. Her order is so complicated I have to ask her to repeat it three times before I get it right. Seriously, why can't people just order a cup of coffee? Why all this *sixteen-ounce quad shot two pump mocha with nonfat milk in a twenty-ounce cup with a lid and two straws* nonsense?

"Hey Clover, can you take this out to the table by the window?" Dean asks, handing me a ceramic mug of black drip coffee. Most customers take theirs to go, but once in a while someone wants to sit with a regular mug. "I'll take the register."

I glance at the guy sitting by the window, and my heart flutters. He's really good-looking. And sitting alone. His dirty-blond hair is kind of messy, and he's wearing these adorable nerd glasses. He's sitting with his headphones hooked to his laptop, his eyes intent on the screen.

"You bet," I say, with slightly more enthusiasm than

necessary. I take the cup and hold it with as much care as I can possibly muster. It's hot, but the tips of my fingers are pretty impervious to heat at this point. I've worked in a lot of coffee shops—it tends to happen.

I navigate my way past the never-ending line of customers toward his table, trying not to let the coffee slosh out. He looks up as I approach, and I give him my friendliest smile.

"Here you go." I slide the mug onto the table, breathing out a sigh of relief. Oh thank God, I didn't spill. He doesn't bother removing his headphones, just gives me a little nod and turns back to his screen.

Well, that's disappointing. But at least I didn't drop his coffee. I managed to break a blender yesterday, and last week I dropped a whole tray of mugs, shattering four of them. I don't know why these things happen to me. I swear, sometimes I'm sure the universe is out to get me.

I turn around to go back behind the counter, and crash into a customer. My eyes widen as most of the iced blended green tea latte he's carrying slides down my front, drenching my boobs.

"Oh no. I am so sorry."

The cup is smashed between us and green slush covers his white shirt. His mouth is wide open and he stares at me.

I cringe. "Please, let me fix this." I run over to the counter and grab a handful of napkins. He stands in one spot, as if the drink froze him solid. The ice in my bra burns my skin, and I'm keenly aware of everyone in the café staring at me—even Mr. Good-Looking Headphones Guy. I try to mop up the damage, but the customer glares at me and steps away.

"Just, don't," he says.

Dean comes out, a fresh drink already in his hand. "Sir, I

am so sorry. Here, we'll of course pay for dry cleaning. And have a gift card as well." He hands the customer the drink and the gift card, shooting me a glare in the process.

Tears sting my eyes, and I back away. I want to go hide. A guy in line snickers, putting a hand to his mouth. The woman behind him gives me a look of pity. I sniff, forcing down the lump in my throat, and go to the back to clean up.

I grab a roll of paper towels and shove one down my shirt. I have green tea everywhere. This bra is a goner. Hopefully Dean will let me go a little bit early. My shirt is soaked, clinging to my skin. Even with my apron on, I can't face customers like this.

"Clover," Dean says. "Can I see you in my office?"

My tummy rolls over. That does not sound good.

"Yeah." I pat my shirt with another paper towel, but at this point it's pretty much futile.

Dean has a little office at the back of the store, not much more than a closet. There's enough space for a small computer desk and one chair in front of it. I've been in this office several times—the first, when I interviewed, was a nice experience. I'm awesome at interviews. They're usually really fun.

The other times, not so much. The blender. The broken mugs. There was another mishap, but I can't remember now what it was. I've only been working here for about three months, and already I've had more than my share of in-the-boss's-office meetings. I sit down across from him, chewing on my lower lip. I was so sure this café is where I'm supposed to be. The signs were all there. Why did it go so wrong?

"Clover, you're a sweet girl."

Oh great, here we go.

"But you're ... well, you're accident prone. I don't know if you're just careless, or if you don't have a good sense of the space around you. But we're a little shop, we don't have a lot of room. Our baristas have to be able to navigate around each other without constantly running into things. And people."

I do not constantly run into things. Just ... once in a while.

"This is the second time you've spilled on a customer," he continues.

Is this the second time? It can't be. No, wait. It is the second time. "Dean, I'm so sorry. I was being so careful with the other guy's coffee, and that dude was right there behind me."

"Yes, but this isn't the first time we've had problems with you. I hate to do this, but I don't think our café is a good fit for you."

I slump back in my seat and look at the floor. Fired? "Are you sure? I'll work on it, I swear. Dean, I really need this job."

Dean sighs. "I'll give you a week's pay, but that's the best I can do."

I bite my lip so my eyes stop tearing up. "Okay, well, thanks for the opportunity."

I get up and don't look back to see Dean's face. I don't want to see him feeling sorry for me. I leave his office, grab my things, and go out the back door.

2

CLOVER

The walk home makes me feel considerably better. Yeah, I was fired, but I didn't like that job anyway. I'll just have to find another one. It's not the first time I've found myself in transition. Not by a long shot.

I ignore the stares of the people passing by. My bra is showing through my damp white t-shirt, the smear of pale green running down to the hem. There isn't anything I can do about it—the weather is warm, so I didn't wear a coat, and I had to leave my apron at the café. I just need to get to my apartment, shower, and figure out what to do next.

The sun shines, and a little trickle of sweat runs down my back. It's a hot one. When I crossed the border into Washington state last year, I expected to drive into a rainy, green forest. It turns out the eastern side of the state is dry, not terribly green, and hot in the summer. I picked the town of Walla Walla because the Internet said it was in Washington's wine country—and come on, who could resist that name?

Wine country turned out to be less romantic than it sounded when I was five hundred miles away, but there are good things about this town. The shops are cute, and I didn't have trouble finding a job. Keeping one is another story, but that isn't my fault—although I can't help but wonder if maybe I should try a new line of work. Or go to school.

After high school, college seemed pointless. My parents didn't go to college, and did fine for themselves. Granted, we moved around a lot, and neither of them had what you'd call a career. And then they went and moved to Thailand the day after I turned eighteen.

But they're free spirits. We spent most of my childhood living in an RV, not owning much of anything, moving from place to place. It wasn't a typical way to grow up, but there's nothing typical about my family.

I miss them sometimes. I haven't seen my parents in years.

I turn into the parking lot of my apartment building. Flower pots spill fragrant blooms, and there's a little playground in the center. It isn't a bad place to live. My upstairs neighbors are night owls, which is a bummer, but I absolutely adore Mrs. Berryshire, the little old lady who lives in the unit next door. As usual, she's sitting in an old rocking chair right outside her door, dressed in a pale pink bathrobe, with curlers in her white hair.

"Hi, Mrs. Berryshire."

"How's my sweet Clover doing today?"

"You know what, I wasn't having such a good day, but everything will be fine."

"You bet it will, sweetie. You want a cookie? I made cookies."

"Oh, no thanks, Mrs. Berryshire." I learned within the first few hours of living here that you never eat Mrs. Berryshire's cookies. Her vision isn't the best, and she tends to mix up ingredients—like salt and sugar.

"All right then. Let me know if you change your mind."

"I sure will."

I smile as I unlock my door. My day is already looking up. I can take a nice hot shower, put my aching feet up, and see if I can find any job postings online. I figure I'll find something by next week. Maybe I'll try for something different this time—like a job that doesn't involve so many breakables and liquids.

I set my bag on the floor and flip the light switch. Nothing happens. That's weird. I try to turn the light on and off a few times, but it doesn't work. The light bulb must be burnt out.

The light in the kitchen also doesn't turn on. I look at the clock on the microwave. It's dark. A feeling of dread creeps through me. The fridge is still cold, but the light there doesn't work either. I walk through my apartment, trying to turn things on, but nothing responds.

Oh no.

I poke my head out the front door. "Hey, Mrs. Berryshire, do you have power in your apartment?"

"I think so."

"Do you mind if I check?"

"Sure thing, sweetie."

I step into her apartment, and all the lights are on. She definitely has power. I do a quick run-through of her place, turning off most of her lights. She tends to forget things like that.

"Yours work," I say when I came out. "I wonder what's wrong with mine?"

"Call maintenance."

"Yeah." I give her another smile. "Maybe the breaker is out or whatever."

I go back inside and grab my phone to call the manager.

My basket of unopened mail catches my eye. That's a pretty big stack. I paid my electric bill, didn't I? I'm sure I did.

I put down my phone and go through the mail. My heart falls down to my toes. I find an envelope with a red PAST DUE stamp on the front. How did I miss that? I open it to find a very overdue electric bill with a disconnect date. Yep, that's today. I guess they really meant it.

I sigh, and set the bill down. I know I have to deal with it, but first things first—I'm still sticky from green tea latte. Hoping I still have a little hot water, I go into the bathroom and turn the shower on. It gets warm, so I risk it. The water never gets very hot, but at least it isn't freezing. I clean up, get out, and put on some fresh clothes.

I check my bank balance to make sure I have enough to cover the electric bill and call the utility to make the payment. They tell me my power should be back on in a few hours. I groan. Hours? I guess it's my fault for getting behind in the first place.

Sitting around with no power is depressing, so I grab my laptop and head to a little Greek restaurant down the road. It's such a great place, and I'm pretty sure they have Wi-Fi. The host shows me to a table by the front window and I order an appetizer. I'll have to make do with pita bread and hummus for dinner; it's one of the cheaper things on the menu. Until I get a new job, I need to be careful with my money. I fire up my laptop, intending to look for a job.

I check social media first, because why not? I've had a long day and deserve a little time to unwind. Then I check my horoscope.

Today, change is in the air. You will be faced with important decisions that will have long lasting consequences for your life—especially your love life. Now is the time to ride the wave of change, let the breeze carry you somewhere new. Don't be surprised if this leads you to an unexpected place, either physically or emotionally. Your optimistic nature will serve you well today.

I stare at the screen. A sign. I always know them when they appear. Sometimes they're in my horoscope. Other times I've seen signs in the clouds, in the stars, in the headlines of magazines. A deep feeling of purpose will steal over me, and I'll *know*. This one means something. I've been following my signs for years—to what end, I'm not sure. But I'm positive they're leading me somewhere great.

Okay, they've mostly led me in circles as I've zig-zagged across the country over the better part of the last ten years, moving from town to town. But I've met the most amazing people, so I can't regret it.

People like Mrs. Berryshire, for example. I wouldn't have met her if I hadn't come to Washington. And there have been plenty of others. I've left behind a string of interesting people, all with great stories.

But as nice as this town is, fate is positively screaming at me right now. Losing my job, my lights being turned off, this horoscope. *Change is in the air. Long lasting consequences. Unexpected place. Ride the wave of change.*

Ride the wave. Waves. That means something, I just know it. I say those words again in my mind and I feel the tingle. It means I'm close to having a breakthrough, that fate is speaking to me. I take a deep breath and close my eyes. What does it mean? What is the universe trying to tell me?

I open my eyes and the first thing I see is a painting of water, sparkling blue in the sun. Waves. It's probably the Mediterranean, and I'm not about to pack up and move to Greece—regardless of how good the food is. But water. The ocean.

I've traveled most of the way across the country, but I've

never seen the Pacific. I bring up a map on my laptop and run my finger down the coast. It's probably only six or seven hours away, and I've been meaning to go there.

Is it time?

I do a search for towns on the Washington coast and click on the second result. I never click on the first. One isn't one of my lucky numbers. But two—two means a couple, and a couple means a future, and a future is what I'm looking for.

Jetty Beach. It looks like a quaint little tourist town. There are cafés, and shops, and long sandy beaches. They won't be warm beaches, but still, it sounds cozy. Quirky. I like quirky—that fits me well.

My worries about my job, my apartment—all of it—fall away in an instant, and a big smile crosses my face. I know. This is where I'm supposed to go. Maybe fate has been leading me to the edge of the country all these years, and I just haven't quite made it yet. After all, where else can I go once I reach the coast? That must be where I'm destined to be.

I close my laptop, finish up my meal, and head to my apartment to pack. I'll leave the furniture. Most of it was here when I moved in anyway. I'll stow the rest of my stuff in my car, and leave first thing in the morning. A heady sense of excitement runs through me. A fresh start. New possibilities. New people. I'll miss my friends here, but it's time, and I have a feeling my horoscope is going to be spot-on.

Change is in the air, and I'll ride the wave where it takes me.

3

CODY

"Dr. J, can you see a walk-in patient? We're slammed and Addy already went home."

I look up from my desk. Darcy, my front desk manager, stands in my office doorway. Her brow is furrowed. She looks stressed.

It's almost six, and I should have left the clinic already. "What's the issue?"

"Five-year-old girl. The mom brought her in, says she won't use her right arm. She's in a lot of pain. If I send them to the ER, they'll wind up waiting longer."

I'm going to be late, but there's no way I won't take this patient. "Yeah, of course."

"Exam room five."

As soon as I open the door, I can see the mom is anxious. Her daughter is in her lap, arm tucked against her body. The little girl's eyes are red-rimmed, her cheeks splotchy.

"Hi. I sit down on the rolling stool so I'm closer to the little girl's level and don't appear so intimidating. "I'm Dr. J. What's your name?"

The mom gives me a tense smile, and the girl looks at me from the corner of her eye.

"Her name is Lily," the mom says. "I'm Christie."

"What's going on, Lily?"

"My arm hurts."

I tilt my head and look at how she's holding it. "Your arm hurts? That's no good. Did you fall down?"

"No," Lily says.

I meet Christie's eyes.

"She didn't fall that I know of. But I might have missed something. She was playing in the living room with her brother while I was cooking dinner, so I didn't see what happened."

"Okay," I say. "Lily, how old is your brother?"

"Eleven."

"Eleven? Wow, he must be pretty big. Do you like playing with him?"

"Yes," she says.

"How old are you?" I ask. "Seventeen?"

She cracks a smile. "No, I'm five."

"Five? Wow, I was way off. Listen, Lily, can you help me out with something?"

She nods.

"I need you to show me your arm. I want to see if I can help it feel better. Can you do that for me?"

She buries her face in her mom's chest.

"She's afraid she's going to get a shot," Christie says.

I nod. "Lily, how about this. I'll make you a promise. No shots, okay? I promise, I will not give you a shot today."

She turns to look at me, still clinging to her mom. "You promise?"

"Yes. In fact, let's pinky promise." I hold out my pinky.

She reaches out her other arm and clasps her tiny pinky

finger around mine. I make a show of shaking up and down a few times.

"Good. Now, I need to touch your arm, okay? I'm going to try really hard not to make it hurt."

She sits still and I very gently probe her arm, starting at her hand. "So you didn't fall down. Your mom said you were playing with your brother. Is that when it started to hurt?"

"Yes," she says.

I touch her elbow and try to move her arm, but she winces, so I stop.

"What were you playing?"

"We were playing ninjas and I had a sword and he tried to take it away."

"Do you like playing ninja?" I'm pretty sure I know what's wrong, so I keep her talking and carefully touch her elbow again. Yep, it's dislocated.

"We always play ninja," she says. "But he wouldn't let me keep the sword."

"Did he pull it out of your hands?"

"Yeah, and he grabbed my arm and pulled really hard."

I meet Christie's eyes. "Lily's elbow is dislocated. It's not an emergency, but I'm sure it hurts. I can pop it back in right now."

Lily's eyes widen. "No, you can't touch it. My arm hurts."

"I know, sweetie. But it's going to stop hurting if you let me fix it for you."

Her lower lip trembles.

"Tell you what." I get a basket of lollipops out of the cupboard; I keep them for just this type of situation. "You take one of these and put it in your mouth, then tell me what flavor it is, okay?"

She still looks suspicious, but nods and takes one. She unwraps the candy and sticks it in her mouth.

I hold her wrist and elbow and quickly rotate the joint back in place. There's a slight snap, and her eyes get big.

"Ouch!"

At first Lily looks at me like I betrayed her trust, but then she moves her arm back and forth, bending it at the elbow.

"Better?"

She nods. "It still hurts, but I can bend it!"

"That's normal. It will feel much better by tomorrow." I look at Christie. "It's a very common childhood injury. The fact that she's moving it now is a great sign. Go ahead and give her a dose of Tylenol before bed if she says it's sore, and it might be tender for a couple of days. But other than that, she should be fine."

Christie's shoulders slump and she lets out a long breath. "Thank you so much, Dr. J. I was so worried it was broken, but I couldn't imagine how she did it."

"It's no problem. But, Lily, you didn't tell me what flavor you got."

Lily smiles. "Bubblegum."

I grin back at her. "That's my favorite. You go see Darcy at the front desk and she'll have a sticker for you, okay?"

"Thank you," she says.

"Yes, thank you so much," Christie says.

"Of course. You two ladies have a wonderful evening."

I head back to my office, well aware that I'm late. But I still have charting to catch up on. When I was in medical school, they somehow left out the part about all the paperwork. I went into medicine because I was attracted to the idea of healing, of helping people—and I admit, the prestige of earning the title *Dr. Jacobsen* doesn't hurt. But this endless paperwork, whether it's on paper or on my computer, is a drag.

I decide I'll just have to come in early tomorrow. I'm

supposed to have dinner with Jennifer. Ostensibly, she's my girlfriend, although it seems like we broke up again the other day. Lately, I'm never sure if we're together or not. She's usually mad at me for working late, and threatens on a regular basis to leave me for good.

Although she owns her own business, too, somehow she doesn't put in the long hours that I do at my practice, and she expects me to be around when she wants me. She calls me a workaholic, and accuses me of not caring about her. I apologize, and we have sex, only to do it all over again a week later.

It's pretty awful, when I think about it. The problem is, I don't think about it. I get up early, go to work, see an endless stream of patients all day, take care of charting and business stuff, and go home late. This mess of a relationship simply isn't a priority to me—which is exactly why Jen is mad all the time.

She's right. I *am* a workaholic.

I shut down my computer and let out a heavy sigh. Workaholic or no, I know that Jen and I have been over for a long time. I need to deal with this once and for all. My brothers have been nudging me, telling me I need to make a clean break. They're right. I've avoided this for way too long.

I don't bother going home to change, instead pulling up at the restaurant still dressed in my cream-colored button-down and blue tie. I find Jen sitting at the bar, her manicured nails tapping against the side of a glass of red wine.

"Really, Cody?" Her straight, dark hair hangs past her shoulders, and she's wearing a black sheath dress and heels.

"Sorry, I got caught up at work. I had a little girl with a dislocated elbow."

"Of course you did," she says with a shake of her head. "I didn't bother getting a table yet, since I knew you'd be late."

My brow furrows. Really? Not an ounce of compassion for a little kid? "Look, Jen, we need to talk."

"Fine, let's just get our table and order. I didn't have lunch and I'm starving."

The host appears before I can say anything else. "I have a table this way, if you're ready."

I follow Jen to a table. It's quiet tonight, not many other customers in the little restaurant. We take our seats and the host hands us menus, but I put mine down and wait for the host to walk away. I'm not going to sit here and eat a meal with her. I'm getting this over with, now.

"Jen, I need to say something."

She keeps looking at the menu. "Sure."

"I think we should finally call it quits."

Her eyes lift to mine, her expression blank. She wears a lot of makeup. "What?"

"We keep doing this. We fight, then we make up, then we fight again, and it's always the same stuff. I'm tired of it."

"You are *not* breaking up with me." She says it with such disdain, it pisses me off.

"Yes, that's exactly what I'm doing. I should have done this a long time ago." I stand up.

Her mouth drops open. "Cody, you can't be serious."

"I'm very serious." Now that I've said it, the rightness of it is so obvious. I'm an idiot for letting this drag out for so long. "We're terrible together, Jen. We make each other miserable. It's like we keep coming back to it because we're afraid there isn't another alternative. But this isn't working. It never really did. This is it. I'm done."

I can feel her eyes boring through my back as I walk away. But fuck it, I don't want to do this anymore. If we get back together tonight, we'll only be fighting again in a few days.

It's amazing how free I feel as I walk to my car. I didn't appreciate how much that shitty relationship was weighing me down.

I get in the car and pick up some Chinese takeout on my way home. My place is about a mile from downtown—not on the beach, but within walking distance. It's a pretty standard two-story, with three bedrooms upstairs, a nice kitchen, and a gas fireplace in the living room. It has a big backyard, and there are plenty of trees for privacy. I bought a newer home, knowing I wouldn't have a lot of time to fix things up, and it's also a lot more space than I need, living here by myself.

But I bought it with the future in mind. I always assumed I would get married and have a family. I'm frustrated with myself for wasting the last couple of years. I knew early on that Jennifer wasn't the one. Why did I stay with her so long?

I go inside, grab a beer, and plop down on the couch with my dinner. I'll eat out of the takeout boxes—no Jennifer to complain and tell me to use a plate. Man, I'm glad she never moved in. She talked about selling her condo and moving in with me, but I resisted. We fought about that, too. It's a good thing I stood my ground. Although now my house seems too big and empty. I haven't done much decorating, even though I've lived here for several years. Yet another thing I put off while I focused on my career.

Dinner is good, and the beer is better—but breaking up with Jennifer means I need to face some harsh truths. She wasn't nice about it, but she is right about my tendency to work too much. I'm busy building my practice, and I'm passionate about what I do. But I know I need better balance in my life.

I'm not sure what to do about it, though. I go to the

kitchen and grab another beer. My younger brother Ryan is getting married next summer, and here I am, starting over. I know I don't want to be the guy who wakes up one day and realizes he's an old man, and all he's done is work. As much as I love what I do, I want more in my life. I don't know what, necessarily. But at least now if it comes along, I'll be open to it.

4

CLOVER

My phone app said the drive would take six hours and twenty-three minutes. Eight and a half hours later, I'm still on the road. The pass across the mountains was backed up for miles. I never saw why.

It's been a really long day, stuffed into my Honda Civic with everything I own in the world, but I'm determined to make it to Jetty Beach before I stop. I have no idea where I'll stay or what I'll do when I get there, but that isn't too important. Fate is leading me. I'm sure something will work out.

I turn up the music and sing along. This part of the state is as green as I imagined it would be. Wide expanses of evergreen trees are everywhere. Even the cities I drive through have a lot of greenery. For the last couple of hours, I've been passing through a series of small towns along the highway, with big gaps between them. I wonder about all the people who live out here. What do they do for a living? Did they grow up here? What are they like?

Finally, I turn a corner, passing a big gateway sign that reads *Welcome to Jetty Beach*. Below that are the words *the ocean is calling ... answer the call.*

A chill runs down my spine. The ocean *is* calling. I can feel it. I need to see the beach. I follow the signs through town and go down a short dirt road with rolling sand dunes on either side, then stop at the end and roll down my window. The waves crash against the sand with a rhythmic roar, and cool, salty air wafts in. I close my eyes, a deep sense of contentment running through me. I made it.

I haven't eaten much except gas station snacks all day, but I decide shelter should come first. This place has a ton of hotels, so I'm sure I'll find something.

Or, not.

It's a Friday, in the middle of summer, and everything is booked. I don't try the fancy-looking ones—I know I can't afford them, even if they have a room available. But all the places that look reasonable are full. I ask at every front desk if they can recommend another, and one sweet lady even calls several other places for me, hoping to find a room. Nope. She strikes out, too.

Food works its way back to the top of my priority list. I don't know where I'll sleep, but I suppose there are worse things than spending a night or two in my car. Maybe the town will clear out on Sunday and there will be more rooms available. Maybe I can secure a job by then. If it's the busy season, I bet there are places hiring.

Yep, everything is still good. The hotel situation is a bump in the road, nothing more. I don't mind a bumpy ride.

I pick a restaurant at random and go inside. It's a *please seat yourself* kind of place, so I choose a small table. A waitress comes by and hands me a plastic menu. Most of the other tables are taken, and the poor thing looks tired.

She brings me some water and I order fish tacos. People-watching is one of my favorite pastimes, so I gaze at the other patrons while I wait for my food. I love to make up stories about the people I see. I doubt I'm ever right about them, but it's a fun way to amuse myself.

I imagine the older couple across from me just learned they're expecting their first grandchild, and they're out to dinner to celebrate. The couple with two little boys is vacationing here on their fifth anniversary, wishing they had brought a babysitter. The teenagers at that table are all about to move away and go to college, so they're having one last night out together before they go their separate ways.

At another table is a young woman, probably about my age, along with three men. I can see her casting admiring glances at the ring on her finger, and the guy sitting next to her puts his arm around her. I bet he's her fiancé. I imagine that they're planning a wedding, and they came to town to take care of details. The two guys with them are their friends, and their girlfriends or wives have gone to the bathroom. They must be the wedding party.

One of the men stands, and I catch a glimpse of his face. He smiles at the others, his dimples showing beneath a light beard. His dark hair is neatly trimmed and he's wearing a perfectly fitting button-down shirt, his body muscular and trim. Now that I look at him, he has to be the other guy's brother. The family resemblance is unmistakable.

I swallow hard. He isn't just attractive. I've seen plenty of attractive men—even dated a few. This one is exquisite. I cannot stop myself from staring as he walks to the back of the restaurant toward the restrooms.

The waitress brings my food and I gasp, blinking at her.

"This looks wonderful."

She gives me a weak smile. "Let me know if you need anything else."

Can you tell me who that guy was? "I'm good, thanks."

She leaves and I watch the table. Mr. Delightful

Dimples comes back and sits across from the couple. My shoulders slump. No women have come out of the bathroom. Maybe it's a double date, but his date is the guy sitting next to him.

I sigh. It figures a guy that beautiful is gay. Oh, well.

I turn my attention back to my dinner. The fish tacos are delicious.

I cast a few more glances at the hot guy at the table. The four of them laugh a lot, and the woman is really pretty. They look like they'd be fun to hang out with, and I find myself wishing I know who they are. My table for one suddenly feels awfully lonely.

I finish up and go to the restroom to splash some water on my face—I'm not sure when I'll have a chance to shower again. I think about asking the waitress if she knows of any other hotels, but she's really busy, so I just pat down my curls a little and head back out the door.

Mr. Delightful Dimples looks up right when I walk out. My eyes lock with his, and he draws his eyebrows together, making a sexy little furrow between his eyebrows. My heartbeat speeds up and I gasp in a little breath. He doesn't look away. Should I smile? Should I say hello? Should I run away?

I take a step forward and slam into something solid. Blinding pain shoots through my head, and my legs crumple as my vision goes dark.

My eyes flutter open. A circle of faces looks down at me, but the only one I can focus on is Mr. Delightful Dimples.

"Hey," he says, his gentle voice full of concern. "Stay with me. Can you open your eyes?"

His hand is behind my neck, holding my head. I nod, wincing at the stabbing pain coming from my forehead.

"Ow."

"Don't move. What's your name?"

"Clover."

"Clover? What's your last name?"

"Fields."

His dimples pucker with his grin. "Your name is Clover Fields? Are you sure?"

"My parents were hippies."

"All right, Clover." His eyes travel up to my forehead and his other hand touches my head softly.

I try not to wince again but it hurts.

"I'm a doctor. You took a pretty bad blow to the head. I'm concerned you might have sustained a concussion."

Oh my god. I hit my head and passed out. "What did I hit?"

"You crashed into a waiter. He was carrying a tray of food up on his shoulder and I think your head hit the edge of the tray. You must have hit pretty hard. You lost consciousness for a few seconds."

I groan. I want to die right here. How many people were watching? Dozens? This is awful.

"Listen, I want to take you to my clinic and check you out, okay? I need to make sure you're all right before I let you go."

I gaze into his gorgeous green eyes. "I'll go anywhere with you." *What did I just say?* "I mean, sure. That's probably for the best."

He grins at the guy who looks like him, who's part of the group standing over me, then looks back at me. "Do you think you can stand?"

"I think so."

He grabs my hands—his are so strong—and helps me to my feet. A few of the other patrons clap.

I smile and give a little wave. "I'm okay."

He takes my arm, as if he's afraid I won't be able to walk, and leads me outside. I'm a little unsteady on my feet. The people from his table follow behind us.

"Here," the woman says, handing me my purse. "You dropped this."

"Thank you. I'm such a klutz."

"Well, I'm Nicole. I hope you're okay. Cody will take good care of you. Promise."

Mr. Delightful Dimples holds out a hand. "Sorry, I'm Cody Jacobsen."

I shake his hand, if only to feel him touch me again. "Clover Fields."

"Yeah, you said that already."

"Oh, sorry."

The guy who looks like Cody steps up beside Nicole. "You got this, Cody? Do you want us to come to the clinic?"

"No, I don't think you need to do that," Cody says. "I'll catch up with you later."

"Text me and let me know how she is," Nicole says.

Cody nods. "I will."

The third guy, the one I thought might be Cody's boyfriend, waves as he walks away. "If you've got this, I gotta run. Later, man."

"See you, Hunter," Cody says. "If you see Mom, just ... you know, be casual."

Well, that doesn't sound gay at all. Are they brothers?

Hunter laughs. "Right. Take care, Clover. Hope your head is okay."

"Thanks."

Cody turns back to me. "Look, I know this is kind of

awkward because you don't know me, but I'm not comfortable letting you drive with a head injury. Can I drive you? My clinic is just up the road. I swear, I'm not a serial killer or anything."

I feel so dazed and out of it. For a second, I think maybe I should be more cautious. Just because he's gorgeous, doesn't mean I should automatically trust him. But my gut is telling me this is fine.

"Here." He pulls out his wallet and hands me a business card. "I'm really a doctor. This is my clinic."

Dr. Cody Jacobsen, Jetty Beach Family Practice.

"You really don't have to do this. I, um … I don't have insurance or anything."

He puts a hand on my elbow. "Don't be silly. I wasn't going to charge you. Come on. You look pretty disoriented."

I am disoriented, but I'm not sure if it's from the knock to the head, or the man standing in front of me. His hand on my arm is making me all tingly.

He keeps a firm grip on my arm and walks me to a sleek black BMW sedan. He opens the door for me, and helps me into the passenger's seat. I settle back into the soft leather.

Cody gets into the car and backs out of his parking space. As soon as the car moves, my stomach rolls over. I clamp a hand to my mouth. Oh, no. I am not going to throw up in this nice man's beautiful car.

"Do you feel like you're going to vomit?" There's no alarm in his voice—just the straightforward question. "Just take deep breaths through your nose."

I nod, still keeping my mouth covered. Cody casts concerned glances at me, the little divot between his eyes standing out.

"Hang in there, Clover. We're almost there."

5

CODY

I pull into the dark lot of my clinic, parking near the front door. Clover sits next to me, her hand covering her mouth. The welt on her forehead keeps looking worse. I hope she doesn't throw up, although I'm not worried about my car. I'm worried about her. Vomiting after a head injury can be a symptom of a serious problem, although nausea is a normal response. I'm pretty sure she has a concussion, particularly since she lost consciousness for a few seconds. I was halfway to calling 911 when her eyes fluttered open and she looked at me.

And when she did ... those eyes. They're huge and blue, and she gazed at me with such a mix of confusion and wonder, it made my heart race. Her curly hair was wild around her face—and that smile. It's a traffic-stopping smile, with her full lips and perfect teeth. But it isn't just her features. She looked up at me, flat on her back in the middle of a crowded restaurant, and her smile lit up the entire room.

I help her out of the car, putting a protective arm around

her shoulders, and tell myself I'm only doing this because she's hurt. It's the right thing to do. I'm a doctor, and I took an oath.

But damn it, she's beautiful.

I unlock the door, lead her around the front desk into the first exam room, and flip on the lights.

"Go ahead and sit up here." I help her up onto the exam table. Her eyes are sad and she hugs her arms around herself. I grab a plastic basin from a cupboard and hand it to her. "Just in case."

She takes it with a weak smile. Damn it. I want nothing more than to bring back the light in her eyes.

I wash my hands, put my stethoscope around my neck, and grab an otoscope and its attachments.

"How are you holding up?" I ask.

"I don't know."

"Any changes to your vision?"

"No, I don't think so."

"What state are we in?"

"Washington."

"Good. Do you have a middle name?"

"Yes. Sunshine."

I stop. Of course her middle name is Sunshine.

"Hippie parents," she says with a little shrug.

"It suits you."

Her expression softens and some of the spark returns to her eyes.

I take one of my scopes and use it to check her pupils. I hold up a finger next to my ear. "Look here."

Her pupils dilate properly, and her eyes look fine. I still need to make sure her memory isn't compromised.

"Do you remember how we got here?"

"Yeah, you drove."

"And how about your head. How did that happen?"

A little flash of confusion crosses her face. "I ... honestly, I'm not sure. You said I ran into a waiter, but I don't remember that. All I remember is..." She trails off.

"What?"

"The last thing I remember is you."

I grab a blood pressure cuff. "Me? That was after you hit your head."

"No, I saw you sitting at your table when I came out of the bathroom. The next thing I knew, I was on the floor."

I know exactly what she's talking about. She came out of the restroom and hit me like a lightning strike. Our eyes met and I felt this crazy sense of foreboding. Like something huge was about to happen. And then, of course, she walked into that waiter.

"Well, what do you expect when you go toe-to-toe with a waiter's tray?" I ask.

She rewards me with a soft laugh.

I push up her sleeve, holding her arm out so I can put on the cuff. Her skin is silky smooth. *Keep it professional, Cody.* But fuck, touching her skin is making me hard. This is so bad.

Her blood pressure is a little elevated, but nothing alarming. I check her ears and carefully probe the bruise on her forehead. It's swelling, which is to be expected, and I get her a small cold pack to hold on it.

I put my stethoscope in my ears and hold the chestpiece up, hesitating. I should not want to touch her like this in the middle of an exam, but there's nothing to do except get it over with. I place a hand on her back and gently hold the chestpiece just below her collarbone so I can listen to her heart. It beats with a steady rhythm. I move the chestpiece lower and listen again, trying to ignore the fact that my hand is close to her breasts. My own heart pounds so hard I'm pretty sure she can hear it.

I clear my throat and pull the stethoscope out of my ears, leaving it to dangle down my chest. "Heart sounds fine. Where do you live?"

"Um, I don't really know."

I look at her in alarm. She can't remember where she lives? That isn't good. "You don't know where you live?"

"Well, not exactly. Until this morning I lived in an apartment in Walla Walla. But I moved out and drove here."

"Oh, I see." She must not have gone to her new place yet. "Did you just get into town today?"

"Yep. I've been here a whole four hours."

"So where's your new place? I take it you haven't moved in yet, since you've been so busy taking dangerous blows to the head."

"Um, no. What I meant is, I don't have a new place."

"You drove here from Walla Walla without a place to stay?"

"Sure," she says with a shrug. "This is a tourist town, I figured I'd find a hotel once I got here. I'll need at least a few days to find a job and a place to live."

I stare at her. "You just showed up in town with no job and nowhere to live?"

Those liquid blue eyes gaze at me. "Uh huh."

I'm not sure what to think of that. I can't fathom doing something so spontaneous. "Well, it's a Friday in the middle of summer. There won't be any rooms available."

"Yeah, I discovered that this afternoon. I went everywhere."

"So, you're telling me you have nowhere to stay tonight?"

Her eyebrows lift. "Well, no, but that's not so bad. I figure some rooms will open up by Sunday and then I'll be fine."

My mouth drops open. "What were you planning to do, sleep in your car?"

"Something like that, yeah."

"No." I shake my head. "You are not sleeping in your car."

"It's okay. I spent most of my childhood living in a big RV. I'm used to sleeping on wheels."

I rub the back of my neck. This is probably a mistake, but there's no way I'm leaving her to sleep in her car.. I'm in grave danger of crossing a line with her as a patient. But she isn't *actually* a patient. Not technically.

"Why don't you come crash at my place?" Her eyes widen and I put up a hand. "I know, you just met me. But you have a head injury. The fact that you lost consciousness, even for a few seconds, is pretty bad. You seem to be doing all right, but your symptoms could get worse. What you need is to lie down and minimize brain activity for at least several days, maybe a week—dark room, no reading, computer use, or TV, and certainly no driving."

She lowers the cold pack and her eyes shine with tears. They nearly crush me. "I can't lie around for a week. I need a job. I need a place to live. I can't—"

"Hey." I step forward, take the cold pack, and gently hold it to her forehead. "You need to rest so you can heal. If you don't take care of this, you could get worse. I really don't mind. I'll even sleep on the couch downstairs, so you'll feel safe. If you want I'll go sleep at my parent's place across town."

"No, no, no. I'm not kicking you out of your own house."

"Okay, just..." I take a deep breath. "Come home with me

tonight. Get some sleep. We'll see how you feel in the morning, okay? Then we can figure out what to do next."

Her bright blue eyes look up at me, wild blond curls framing her face. Her mouth turns up in that brilliant smile, and I feel like I just won the fucking lottery.

"Okay."

6

CLOVER

Cody's house is gorgeous. A little plain, perhaps, but it has so much potential. He leads me up the stairs to the front porch—all it needs is a nice bench or swing, and it would be completely adorable. Inside are gleaming hardwood floors, a stairwell with a beautiful dark wood banister, and an open living room, dining room, and kitchen. He doesn't have a lot of furniture, just a couch and a dining table with four chairs. The walls are bare and there isn't anything on the kitchen counters. It hardly looks like he lives here.

"You can help yourself to anything," he says, showing me the kitchen. "Although you really need to try to lie down as much as possible. And not too much TV or screen use. Music is fine."

He leads me upstairs. There are three bedrooms, a hall bath, and a closet. The master is furnished, but the other two bedrooms are empty.

"You can have my room tonight." He gestures into the master. "I'll put on clean sheets for you."

"No," I say, emphatic. "You've been so nice to me already. You are not giving up your bedroom."

He takes me by the arm and gently leads me into his room. Oh holy hell, it smells like him in here—subtle but fresh.

"At least for tonight. We'll see how your head is doing in the morning, but I won't take no for an answer."

I would never say no to you. "Honestly, I'm fine."

He takes my shoulders and nudges me so I sit on the edge of the bed. "Are you?"

I'm not. My head is killing me and I still feel sick. I can't quite think clearly. All I really want is to lie down and sleep.

With a gentle hand, he touches my forehead. "The swelling isn't too bad, but you'll have a bump for a few days."

Instinctively, I touch it. "Ouch."

He takes my hand, holding it in his own. I try so hard to control my reaction, but his touch makes me tremble.

"Careful. Don't touch it."

He could drop my hand, but he doesn't. He holds on for a long moment. His closeness makes my heart flutter.

He lets my hand go and clears his throat. "So, I'll get sheets. Do you want something to wear? I guess we should have gone back to your car to get your things. Do you want me to run down there for you?"

"No, it's fine. Please, you've already done way too much for me."

He leaves and comes back with a set of folded sheets and a white t-shirt.

"I don't, um..." he says, looking around. "I probably don't have the toiletries you need, but there's an extra toothbrush, still in the package, in the bathroom. There's regular soap and stuff in the shower, but maybe don't shower tonight. We need to make sure you're not going to lose consciousness again."

"I don't even know what to say." If my head didn't hurt so bad, I would probably jump him, but I really need to lie down.

"Don't say anything, then. Just get some rest. I don't have to work tomorrow, so I'll see you in the morning. If you, um ... if you sleep late, do you mind if I wake you? I kind of want to check on you."

My heart melts into a big, sloppy puddle inside my chest. "Sure." I meet his eyes and smile.

He smiles back, delicious dimples and all.

I move off the bed while he changes the sheets. I kind of don't want him to—the thought of smelling him all night while I sleep is so tempting. But how do you ask something like that? *Thanks, but I'd like to roll around in your dirty sheets, if you don't mind...*

When he finishes, he grabs one of the pillows and an extra blanket out of the closet. "I'll let you get some sleep. The door locks from the inside, if that makes you feel safer."

"I'm fine. I think if you wanted to hurt me, you would have done it already."

He smiles again and a chill runs down my spine. "Good night, Clover."

"Good night."

He leaves, closing the door behind him.

I slump down on the freshly made bed, blowing out a long breath. I grab his t-shirt and hold it up to my face. Oh my god, it does smell like him, a little bit at least. I debate whether I should put it on, or just take off my bra and sleep in my own clothes. I don't know if I can sleep with his scent all over me.

Except I need to stop that kind of thinking. He's been

nothing but an absolute gentleman. Not even a gentleman —a knight. A knight from a fairy tale, not a murdery one with a big sword. And here I am, imagining what he must look like under that adorable button-down shirt.

Stop it, Clover.

I take off my clothes and slip on his t-shirt. It's fresh and clean and just the right size to be big and comfy on me. I lift the neckline and sniff it again as I crawl into his bed. I glance at the door, wondering if I should lock it.

No way. Dr. Cody Jacobsen isn't going to come to me in the middle of the night. He's far too gentlemanly. But if he does, I certainly won't say no.

7

CODY

I stare at the ceiling, not sleeping.

I have no idea what time it is, but it has to be well after two. I'm exhausted, but I can't sleep. I can't convince my dick to calm the fuck down, which is the majority of the problem.

I have the most intoxicating woman I've ever met in my bed, and I'm downstairs, debating whether or not to rub one out while I lie on the couch. That's terrible of me. She's the sweetest woman, and all I can think about is the way she must look wearing my t-shirt. I bet it's just long enough to hang below her ass, brushing the tops of her thighs. And her nipples are probably poking out through the white fabric, her hair unruly around her face.

Stop it, Cody.

I hold one of the throw pillows over my face and groan. I'm not going to be able to sleep with her so close. My hands have a whiff of her perfume on them—she smells faintly of vanilla. It's a warm, comforting scent. I put down the pillow and sniff my hands, not for the first time. I groan again. That is not helping.

How am I going to do this for a week?

There's no doubt she needs to stay. If she argues, I'll find a way to convince her. That head injury is no joke, and I can't in good conscience let her go—especially since she's new in town and doesn't have anywhere else to stay. Maybe I should have taken her to my parents' house, but the truth is I didn't want to. I want her here, crazy as that is—even if she does keep me up all night.

I tell myself it's only so I can check up on her, make sure she's okay. While that's true, I know I'm kidding myself. That isn't the only reason.

It's going to be a long night.

A KNOCK on the door jolts me awake. I rub the sleep from my eyes as I get up from the couch, and stagger to the front door. Apparently I finally fell asleep sometime in the early morning hours, but I'm still tired.

I open the door to find my mother.

"Mom?" I ask, blinking hard.

"Cody," she says, a hint of impatience in her voice. "Did you just wake up?"

"Yeah." I step aside to let her in. She's wearing a long blue dress with a beige cardigan over the top, and she has a reusable shopping bag slung over her arm. "What time is it?"

"It's nine," she says, her voice cheery. "Come on, honey, get dressed."

I look down at myself. I'm not wearing anything except a pair of boxer briefs. "Oh, shit." I turn to the stairs, but remember Clover is in my room. I hurry over to the couch and grab my shirt, slipping my arms through the sleeves.

"What are you doing here so early?" I ask.

"We're going to the farmer's market. Remember? Mother-son date day? You forgot, didn't you?"

I put a hand to my forehead. I did forget. Shit. "Yeah, Mom, I forgot. I'm really sorry. I kind of had a rough night last night."

"Did you sleep on the couch?" She gestures toward the crumpled blanket and pillow.

Shit again. I don't want to explain Clover to her. My mom is literally the nosiest person ever.

"Uh, yeah. Look, Mom, today isn't a good day for me to go to the market. I didn't get a lot of sleep and I haven't showered or anything. Can we do this next weekend?"

She narrows her eyes at me—her interrogation stare. I'm done for. "Why were you sleeping on the couch? Is Jennifer upstairs?"

"No, Jennifer is not upstairs."

"Then why—"

"Mom," I say, interrupting her. "It's nothing. I just fell asleep with the TV on."

"Okay." Clearly, she does not believe me. "Well, I'm sorry we couldn't have our date today. I've been looking forward to spending time with you."

Moms are so good at guilt, and mine is no exception. "I know, Mom. I'm really sorry." *Please go before Clover wakes up.* "I promise, I'll make it up to you, okay?"

"All right, honey." She turns and stops in her tracks. I can't see past her, but I know exactly what she sees.

"Oh, I'm sorry. Um, hi?"

Mom's face swings to me. She has one eyebrow arched. "I see that Jennifer is in fact not upstairs."

"No, she's not. Mom, this isn't the time."

"Are you going to introduce me to your friend?"

Clover steps forward, but her face pales. The welt on her forehead stands out, all purple and red. She's dressed in nothing but my white t-shirt, her legs bare.

Oh, for fuck's sake.

"No, Mom, you don't understand." I stop, rubbing my jaw. How do I explain this to her and not sound like a total lunatic? "This is Clover."

Mom's eyebrows lift even higher. "Clover?"

"Yes, Clover. I was at a restaurant last night and Clover hit her head. I took her back to the clinic to make sure she was okay. She has a concussion, but with some rest she should make a full recovery."

"Then why is she in your house, dressed in nothing but a t-shirt?" There's more bewilderment than judgment in her voice, but Clover still cringes.

"She just moved to town, and she doesn't have anywhere else to go. With a head injury like that, I couldn't let her be alone. So I let her have my room and I slept on the couch."

Mom's expression instantly melts into sympathy. "Oh, honey," she says, turning to Clover. She grabs her hands and gently brushes her curls back from her face. "Look at that bruise. Goodness, my dear, that looks awful. You were so fortunate that my son was there."

"I really was," Clover says with a big smile.

"Aw, sweet thing. "Cody, do you have anything here for a decent breakfast?" She bustles into the kitchen and starts rooting through the fridge and cupboards.

Clover looks at me with wide eyes. I realize I'm still in nothing but my underwear and an open shirt. With my mom in the kitchen.

Shit.

I grab my pants and pull them on as quickly as I can.

Seeing Clover half-naked is waking me up, fast, and I do *not* need my mother seeing my hard-on.

I don't need Clover seeing it either.

"You know what, Mom, I need to see how Clover's injury is doing," I say, guiding her out of the kitchen. "After that, if she's up to it, I'll take her out to breakfast. Or I'll go to the store. We're fine. So, next week for the farmer's market?"

"All right, I can take a hint."

Clover sits down on the couch while I walk my mom to the door. Mom hesitates in the doorway.

"What's going on with Jennifer?" she asks in a whisper.

"I ended it." I cast a quick glance over my shoulder. Clover pulls my blanket up over her lap.

"Well, it was time," Mom says. "I was wondering, because I can't imagine the hell she'd give you if she found out about that sweet girl in there."

"Yeah, I know. But it's fine. And Clover's not ... I was just trying to help."

"You're a good boy." She pats me on the cheek. "Bring her over for dinner when she feels better."

"Mom—"

"No," she says, cutting me off. "You do it. She's new in town. I'm sure she could use some friends. Bring her by. How about Thursday? I'll have everyone over. She should meet Nicole."

I lean against the door frame and rub my eyes again. "Fine, Thursday. If she feels better. She might need more time."

"You're the doctor. Okay, I have to go. I need to call Ryan."

"I don't think you need to keep calling Ryan every day. He has Nicole."

"So?" she asks with a smile, her tone completely genuine.

I smile. "You're right, Mom. Call Ryan."

"Bye, baby boy. I'll see you later."

"Bye, Mom."

I let out a breath and close the door, then go back to the couch and sit down next to Clover.

Thankfully, her legs are tucked up beneath the blanket. "Wow, your mom is so nice."

"Yeah, she's..." I pause, trying not to laugh. "She's something else."

"Did you have plans with her today?"

"I guess I did, but honestly, I'd forgotten."

"I'm so sorry. I took your room, and your bed, and I made you miss plans with your mom. I'm awful."

"No, I would have forgotten the thing with my mom anyway." I push Clover's hair back to look at her forehead. Leaning close, I get another hit of her scent. It's a good thing I'm wearing pants. "I'm happy with how this looks. How are you feeling? Did you sleep okay?"

"It took me a while to fall asleep, but once I did, I slept like a baby. My head hurts though."

"Yeah, it will take some time. Still no vision changes?"

"Nope."

"How's the nausea?"

"Oh, fine. I think I'm just hungry at this point."

"I'll figure out some breakfast. I don't have much here, so I'll run out and get us something."

"You really don't have to do that."

I shrug. "Well, I need to eat, too. Do you drink coffee?"

"Yes. Lots of it."

"Okay, you stay here. Lie down if you don't feel well. I'll

be back. Do you want me to stop by your car and pick up anything?"

Clover pulls the blanket up higher onto her lap. "That's okay. Really, you're doing too much already. I can deal with my stuff later."

I run upstairs and change into jeans and a t-shirt, trying not to look at the rumpled bed. I go back down, grab my keys, and pause at the front door. Clover gives me that vivid smile and waves.

I'm in big trouble.

8

CODY

I drive out to Charlie's Grocery and wander the aisles, grabbing random things. I don't usually keep a lot of food in my house. I work so much, I'm not often home for meals. It was one of the things Jennifer complained about. She even took to buying groceries—things she wanted to have around when she came over—and leaving them at my place. I ignored the way it irked me, but now that she isn't in my life anymore, I'm able to admit how irritating it was. I didn't want to keep her stupid soy milk in my fridge. Soy milk is disgusting.

I have no idea what Clover likes to eat, so I try to include a little bit of everything. Cereal, milk, soup, eggs, bacon, frozen waffles, syrup, hash browns, a carton of strawberries. I'm probably overdoing it. I grab more pain relievers—she's likely to have a perpetual headache for several days, and I can cycle Tylenol and Motrin for her—and throw in some girly-looking shampoo, conditioner, body wash, and something called a loofah that I seem to recall seeing Jennifer use.

Just as I'm heading to the cashier, someone turns their

cart down my aisle. I almost crash into her, and when I see who it is my gut fills with dread.

Jennifer. Of course it's Jennifer.

"Oh, hi." Her perfectly straight hair is shiny, her makeup flawless. Even on a Saturday morning, she's dressed in a blouse, slacks, and heels. She probably doesn't own a pair of jeans.

"Hi, Jennifer," I say, purposely not calling her Jen. No sense in continuing with that familiarity.

"What are you doing here?"

"Is it not obvious? I'm doing the same thing you are. I'm shopping."

"Wow," she says, her voice thick with sarcasm. "You strike out on your own and suddenly you're all responsible."

"I'm glad to see we can be civil when we run into each other." I move my cart to go around her.

"Cody, wait." She puts a hand on my arm as I try to walk by. "We didn't have a chance to talk things over the other night. Why don't we go get some coffee?"

I pull my arm away. "I don't think that's a good idea."

"Why not? Just as friends. We can catch up. You can tell me how things are going with the practice. Anything new there?"

"Nothing new. I have to go."

"What's going on with you?"

"I'm not sure how that's any of your business at this point."

A flash of anger crosses her face. "Oh my god, you're sleeping with someone, aren't you? That's what this is all about."

"As a matter of fact, no, I'm not." *Although I've certainly been thinking about it.* "But if I was, it wouldn't have anything to do with you."

"Yes, it would." She crosses her arms. "You can't just leave me and jump in bed with some slut."

"For fuck's sake," I say, lowering my voice and leaning closer to her. She doesn't know about Clover, but I can't help but feel like she just called her a slut. I'm so angry, I'm having trouble keeping my voice under control. "I can do as I damn well please. You and I were never good together, and I can't even fathom how I put up with you for two years."

I push my cart past her, leaving her gaping at me.

My heart thumps hard in my chest, my body full of adrenaline. I go to an open cashier and pay for my cart full of stuff, getting myself out of the store as quickly as I can. The fresh air helps me calm down. By the time I load my groceries into the trunk of my car, I'm more or less back to normal.

I am not going to let Jennifer get to me.

After a quick stop at Old Town Café for coffee, I go home. I find Clover lying on the couch, her head on my pillow, my blanket up to her chin. She has a plastic bag full of ice on her forehead.

"Oh, hey, don't put that right on your skin." I grab a paper towel and rush over to her.

She opens her eyes and lifts the ice. "What?"

"You want something between the ice and your skin. It's too cold." I take the ice and wrap it in the paper towel, then place it carefully back on her forehead. "There. Better?"

"Yes, thank you."

She tries to get up, but I put a hand on her shoulder and nudge her back. "No, lying down is good."

"But, coffee."

"Fine, coffee, then you lie down."

I grab our two cups and hand one to her. She scoots herself up to sitting and takes a sip.

"Is Jennifer your girlfriend? I heard your mom say something."

Her question catches me off guard. "No. She was, but we broke up. Recently."

"Oh, I'm sorry to hear that."

Is it just me, or does Clover not look sorry? "Don't be. It was long overdue. I'm much better off."

Her face brightens. "Well, that's good then."

My phone dings and I take it out of my pocket to check, hoping it isn't Jennifer. I have a text from Nicole. *How's Clover? Is her head okay?*

I type out a quick reply. *Concussion, but she'll be fine in a few days.* "My soon to be sister-in-law is checking up on you."

"Really?"

"Yeah, you met Nicole at the restaurant last night. She texted to ask how you're doing."

Clover looks genuinely baffled. She puts the ice down on the coffee table. "Wow."

I get another text. *She still at your place?*

I look at the screen again. How does Nicole know? *Um, yes. How did you know she was here?*

Nicole answers. *Your mom called Ryan earlier.*

Of course, my mother.

"Is everything okay?" she asks.

"Yeah, it's fine. Sometimes I forget how quickly news travels in this town."

Clover's hand flies to her mouth and she gasps.

"What's wrong?"

"Oh my god, I'm a criminal."

I don't mean to laugh, but she's so serious. "What do you mean?"

"I never paid for my dinner last night. We left and I didn't pay."

"You're fine. Bob and Diane own the place, and they're really nice people. I'm pretty sure they won't press charges."

She puts a hand to her forehead, then winces. "Ouch."

"Okay, time to lie down."

"I need to go deal with this. And get my car out of their parking lot. I bet it's been towed."

"It hasn't been towed."

She lets out a breath. "Cody, you've been so nice. I really do appreciate everything you've done. More than I can say. But I really need to find a place to live and start looking for a job."

"I know. You will. But you need to heal first."

She scowls. How does she make that look cute?

"Clover," I say, adding some doctor sternness to my tone, "that headache you have is your body telling you to slow down."

"What am I supposed to do? You can't keep sleeping on your couch."

No, but maybe I could join you upstairs.

Stop it, Cody.

"Sure I can."

"Cody—"

"Listen. You're going to stay here with me until you're better. That's my prescription. Rest. Quiet. No stress. Everything else can wait a few days."

"Are you sure?"

"Positive." I take her coffee cup and set it on the table. "Come on, lie down. Doctor's orders."

She flashes me a grin. "All right, Dr. Jacobsen. I'll do whatever you say."

It's hot when she tells me she'll do what I say. I hesitate, watching her as she lies down, overcome with the desire to kiss her. I could lean down slowly, see how she reacts. If she turns away, I could stop. But if she doesn't...

I clear my throat and get up, my cock straining against my pants. What is wrong with me? She's hurt. Vulnerable. I have to quit fantasizing about taking advantage of her.

9

CLOVER

Cody gets my car for me—yet another thing I need to thank him for. As frustrated as I am to be lying down all day, I have to admit, he's right. I need the rest. I can tell when I overdo it. My head aches and the nausea comes back. So I spend a few days lying on his couch and sleeping in his bed. No matter how hard I try to convince him to take his room back, he won't hear of it.

I'm so tempted to ask him to join me in bed. Every evening he says goodnight and I wander up the stairs, wondering if I should just ask. What's the harm in that? We're both single adults. But I can't make myself do it. He's been such a gentleman, it feels wrong.

I swear there are moments when he looks at me as if he wants the same thing. There's a hunger in his eyes. But he always backs off so quickly. Maybe I'm imagining it, and he doesn't want me. I decide that it's best if I don't complicate things.

By Wednesday, I'm going out of my mind—and not just because I bumped my head. I decide it's time to get out of the house. Cody works all day, but I figure I can find my way around. Jetty Beach isn't a big town.

I drive around a bit to get my bearings, then circle back down Main Street. It's so cute, with trees lining the street, and pretty hanging baskets spilling pink, red, and white flowers. I pull into a parking spot—the second one that's open, not the first. I get out and look around. Right in front of me, I see what I'm looking for: a coffee shop.

Cody does not understand coffee, so the supplies at his house are less than ideal. I'm dying for a good cup. Old Town Café looks like just the sort of place to serve the good stuff. I resolve to see if they sell bags of whole beans, and I'll find a good quality grinder and French press. Then I can make it at home.

I roll my eyes. It isn't home. It's Cody's house, and I need to remember that finding a new place to live should be at the top of my list.

The café smells amazing. Fresh coffee, baked goods, and they have a full kitchen. I worked at a café with a full menu once, but despite telling them I can cook, they never let me touch the food.

A pleasant-looking woman in her forties is behind the counter. "What can I get you?"

I look at the case. "Coffee, and a blueberry muffin. Those look amazing."

"We bake them fresh every day," she says, opening the case on her side and reaching in with a napkin to grab a muffin.

"Do you? Yum."

"For here, or to go?"

"I'll stay."

She puts my muffin on a plate and pours my coffee into the cutest ceramic mug. It looks like a chalkboard.

She points to a side table. "Cream and sugar are over there."

"Thank you so much." I hand her the money. "This looks wonderful."

"No problem," she says with a smile.

I pause at the counter. Should I? Why not. "Say, you don't happen to be hiring?"

She tilts her head at me. "I might be."

I smile. I *knew* it. "If you are, I'd love the opportunity to apply."

She grabs a towel and wipes off her hands, her eyes still on me. Is she deciding if I look like Old Town Café material?

"I'm sorry, I don't mean to stare. It's just so odd that you asked that when you did. One of my employees quit not ten minutes ago, and didn't give any notice."

A tingle runs up my spine. It's a sign. "That's not good."

"No, it isn't. She put me in a really bad position. I know you didn't come here prepared to interview, but would you mind sitting down with me over your coffee?"

"I would love to," I say with a smile.

She comes around the counter and we go to a table next to the window. I set my muffin and coffee down and take a seat across from her.

"I'm Natalie," she says, holding out her hand.

"Clover." I take her hand and shake. "And yes, that's my real name, no my parents didn't hate me, but yes they were hippies. My last name is Fields, if you can believe it."

Natalie laughs. "I suppose you get a lot of questions about your name."

"All the time."

"Are you new in town?"

I nod. "I got in last Friday."

"And why did you move to Jetty Beach?"

"It was time for a change," I say with a shrug.

"I can understand that. What about experience?"

"Oh, I've worked in a lot of coffee shops. I've also been a dog groomer, worked in a flower shop, been a hostess at a restaurant, and a few other things." Natalie's eyes look a little wide, so I press on. "I know that makes me sound like a huge flake, but it's just that I've moved around, so I had to get new jobs. Plus, I like trying new things."

"All right. What would you say is your best quality as an employee."

I love this question. "I'm very cheerful, even when customers aren't. I get a lot of compliments on my smile, and my favorite thing is to make other people feel happy."

Natalie smiles at me. "I can see that. What's your biggest challenge, then? What do you struggle with?"

I take a deep breath. I don't want to have to tell her this, but if she asks for a reference from my last job, she's going to find out anyway. "Sometimes I'm a little clumsy. Or maybe a lot clumsy. I wish I didn't have to tell you this, but I don't like being dishonest. I was fired from my last job. I broke some things, and I ran into a customer, spilling an iced blended green tea latte all over him."

Natalie winces. "That's too bad."

"Well, to be fair, it was a really small shop and always super crowded. And I swear, I'll try so hard not to drop anything if you hire me."

"I appreciate your honesty, and if the worst thing about you is that we lose a few mugs, I think we'll be doing fine."

I sit up a little taller and try not to make any squeeing noises.

"If you think you'll be living in Jetty Beach for a while, I'd love to give this a try. "You're very personable and I think you'd fit in really well here. I suppose I should ask how you are at making coffee."

"I make the best coffee in the world." I'm totally and completely serious. I really do.

Natalie smiles at me again. "That settles it, I suppose. When can you start?"

My hand drifts up to the bump on my head. It is so polite of her not to mention it. I figure Cody would say I should wait until next week before I start working, but the sooner I start, the sooner I'll be back on my feet. I figure I'll split the difference. "How about Saturday?"

"Perfect. If you can, come in Friday afternoon. We'll fill out some paperwork, and I can show you around."

"I will, definitely." I'm having a hard time containing myself. "Thank you so much, Natalie. This is amazing."

"Thank you, Clover. I almost feel like this was meant to be."

Oh yes, it's meant to be. "I do too. Thank you."

She leaves me to my coffee and muffin, although I'm not hungry anymore. I'm too excited. I have a job. A job means money, and money means a place to live, and a place to live means I can stay in Jetty Beach. I have to tell Cody.

I leave the rest of my coffee and take my muffin in a to-go bag. I'm not sure where his clinic is, but my mapping app finds it and I drive straight there, passing through the rest of the downtown strip. I already love this town—it's so cute. Maybe Cody and I can go to the beach to celebrate. I practically bounce in my seat, I'm so thrilled.

I go into the clinic and walk up to the front desk. The lady behind the counter is wearing a bright blue blouse and her hair is pulled up in a bun.

"Hi. I need to see Co—I mean, Dr. Jacobsen, please."

"Do you have an appointment?"

"Oh, no, I just want to see if he's available for lunch."

"Is he expecting you?"

"Nope," I say with a smile.

The front desk lady's brow furrows and she glances at a nurse in purple scrubs grabbing something off a printer behind her. "Is Dr. J with a patient?"

"No, he's in his office."

Front Desk Lady picks up her phone and presses a button. "Hi, Dr. J. There's someone out front who would like to see you." She looks up at me. "What's your name?"

"Clover."

She looks even more confused. I don't understand what the big deal is. "She says her name is Clover. Okay, I'll let her know." She puts down the phone. "He'll be right out."

"Thank you," I say with a big smile.

I take a seat in the waiting area and pick up a trashy magazine. They're the best thing about waiting rooms. I thumb through, glancing at the pictures of celebrities in beautiful clothes.

Cody comes through the door next to the front desk. "Clover, what are you doing here? Are you okay?"

I practically drool. He looks so good in his pale green button-down shirt and striped tie, with the stethoscope around his neck. So serious and doctory.

I stand. "Yeah, I'm fine. I'm great, actually. Can you grab lunch?"

"What? No, I have patients to see."

"Oh. Sorry. I thought..."

He glances at Front Desk Lady, who is clearly staring at us. "Let me walk you out."

I'm so surprised, I go out to my car without saying a word. I haven't had a chance to tell him my great news.

He stands next to the driver's side door of my car. "Why are you driving? You should be lying down."

"I'm tired of lying down, and I feel fine. I got a job."

"You what?"

Why is this such a shock? Am I such a disaster that he can't believe I found a job right away? "A job. You know, the thing where you go to work and they pay you?"

"Where?"

"Old Town Café. I went in to get coffee and thought I'd ask. It turned out she had an employee quit just before I got there. It was totally meant to be."

"That's great, Clover," he says, looking back at the door to the clinic.

"So I thought I'd come tell you, and you'd be happy for me, and we could go have lunch. It's noon, and you went to work at like six this morning."

His face shows surprise, and I realize it's probably weird that I know that, given that I was upstairs in his bedroom and should have been sleeping. But I hear him get up and shower in the other bathroom every morning. I always imagine what he looks like naked, and can't get back to sleep.

"I did, but like I said, I have patients to see. I'm happy for you about the job, but you can't just show up here like this."

"Oh, yeah." I look away, feeling awful. Of course he can't just leave. He's a doctor. People put their lives in his hands. "I'm sorry, I didn't think. I was just so excited, I wanted to tell someone. And, well, I don't know anyone else."

His face softens and he touches my arm. I like it when he does that.

"I'm sorry, I'm just really busy today. Congratulations on the job. That's really good news. I'm impressed."

"Yeah?"

"Definitely. You haven't even been here a week, and you managed a head injury and a new job."

I give him a playful smack on the arm. "Okay, go save lives or whatever."

He laughs. "I don't know about that, but I do have to get back. I'll see you tonight, okay?"

"Sure." I open my car door.

"And Clover?"

"Yes?"

"Go lie down. You've had a busy day. Your brain needs rest."

"Yes, Dr. J," I say with a grin.

I get in my car, but I'm not going to head to his place yet. I have a lot of thanking to do, and now that I have a job lined up I don't have to be quite so worried about spending a little money. As much as I want to thank Cody in other ways, I have an idea. I'll make him dinner.

How long has it been since he's come home from work to a hot meal? I wonder if his ex cooked for him. Well, if there's one thing I can do as well as make coffee, it's cook. I'll stop at the grocery store, get ingredients, and make him something fantastic. It's the least I can do after everything he's done for me.

Quite pleased with myself, I drive off to put my plan into action.

10

CODY

Clover's surprise visit sets me on edge. I walk past the front desk, knowing Darcy's eyes are on me. When it comes to gossip, my front desk staff is rivaled only by the nursing staff. They're going to have a field day trying to figure out Clover.

I go back to my office and have just enough time to check my messages before Maria, my nurse, buzzes me to say my next patient is waiting. I bring up the chart on my tablet. Shit. It's Lyle Brown. If he's here, it probably means his treatment isn't working. Which means I'll need to go back to the drawing board.

Lyle is a man in his mid-forties who came to me recently with stiffness and muscle spasms, primarily in his neck, upper back, and shoulders. I followed standard protocol and sent him home with a sedative to help him sleep and muscle relaxers to ease the spasms. I haven't heard from him, so I hoped he was doing better.

I can tell by his face when I enter the exam room that he's not better. "Hi, Lyle. I hope you weren't waiting long."

"No." He winces and his hand clenches a few times.

"Still having trouble?" I swipe across my tablet screen, looking at his chart to refresh my memory. "Last time you had muscle spasms and quite a lot of pain. Is that still the case?"

"Afraid so. I figured I'd just tough it out, but my wife made another appointment."

Thank goodness for wives, or I'd lose half my male patients. "That was the right thing to do. If the treatment isn't working, we need to reevaluate. Have you been taking the muscle relaxers?"

"I have."

"Have you noticed any improvement?"

"No, not really."

That isn't what I want to hear. "Okay, let's have a look."

I check him over, but I'm not sure what I'll find that's new. He's an otherwise healthy, active adult male without any history of medical problems. I can feel his neck muscles contracting, and his back shows signs of acute muscular stress as well. He must be in a lot of pain.

"I'd like to do another blood panel and see if we can start ruling things out. I might need to order additional tests, but I need to see your blood work first. I don't want to put you through anything that isn't necessary. Unfortunately, at this point there are a lot of things that can cause your symptoms. We need to investigate further and start crossing things off that list. Once we narrow it down, we'll know what else to test for. In the meantime, I can give you a different muscle relaxer if the one you're taking isn't providing enough relief. I can prescribe pain relief as well, if you need it."

"Thanks Dr. J. The sleeping stuff you gave me knocks me

out pretty well at night, but I'm struggling during the day. It's hard to work."

"I'll do what I can to help you be more comfortable while we wait on your results. Maria will come back and take some blood, and then I need you to set up a follow-up appointment. Do it before you go, so you don't forget."

"Believe me, my wife won't let me forget. She'll be after me for all the details. She would have come with me, but she had to work."

"I understand. We're going to figure this out. I'll do some research and see what else I can find while we wait for your blood work. Hang in there, okay?"

"Will do, doc."

I send Maria in to take blood and go back to my office. I need a moment to collect myself before my next patient. The only thing worse than losing a patient is watching one suffer and not knowing how to help them. I already looked up a list of possibilities that could account for Lyle's symptoms after his last visit. None of them are good news, and most of them are degenerative. That means he'll keep getting worse if we can't find out what it is, and he might keep deteriorating even if we can. I pinch the bridge of my nose and take a deep breath. I'll do everything I can for him, but I have to put some distance between me and his case—keep my emotions out of it.

The rest of my day goes smoothly. I have a one month well-baby visit, which are among my favorite appointments. The mom is doing wonderfully, and her son is thriving. I see several other children for checkups, as well as a couple sick visits, and one patient with a broken arm. All in all, a pretty typical day at my practice.

I spend time after my last patient finishing up my charts

and taking care of other business, including registering for a medical conference in Portland I've been wanting to attend.

Then I look at the clock and realize it's after seven. I'm starving. I didn't take much time for lunch—just grabbed a quick sandwich from Old Town Café around two. I think about picking something up on my way home, but I'm so tired, I don't want to deal with it. I have food left from my shopping trip, I'm sure I'll find something—even if it's just frozen waffles.

I drive home, and when I open my front door the scent of food hits me. What is that? My mouth waters and my stomach rumbles. It smells amazing.

I find Clover busy in the kitchen. The table is set for two and she's already placed a couple serving dishes in the center, along with a bottle of wine.

She looks up and smiles. Every time she does that, I melt a little.

"Hi," she says.

"What's all this?"

"Dinner," she says with another grin.

"Seriously? This smells unbelievable."

"Are you hungry?"

"I'm famished."

She claps her hands together. "Perfect. I've been trying to keep things warm because I wasn't sure when you'd be home, but I'm pretty sure it's all still good."

I stand motionless while she bustles around the kitchen, bringing the last of the things to the table. I'm stunned. Not only does it look and smell amazing, I can't believe she went to all this trouble.

"Okay, it's ready. Come sit." She pulls out the chair at the head of the table and takes her seat next to me. "We have sautéed asparagus with hollandaise, roasted garlic couscous, lemon grilled chicken, and bacon-wrapped scallops. I wasn't sure what you liked, so I probably made too much."

"This is..." I pause, staring at all the food. "This is incredible."

"Yeah? I wanted to do something nice to show you how grateful I am."

"Thank you." I hope she can hear in my voice how much I mean it. I'm so touched.

"It is absolutely the least I can do. You've done so much more for me than you should have. I'll have to find more ways to make it up to you."

There's a twinkle in her eye and one corner of her mouth turns up. I try to ignore the sudden tingle that runs from my chest straight to my swelling cock. Damn it.

I clear my throat. "You don't have to do anything."

She holds my gaze. "But I want to."

Oh my god.

"Let's eat," she says.

I'm starving, but her tongue darts across her lips and it's all I can do not to reach over and grab her so I can devour that gorgeous mouth.

"Do you eat seafood?" she asks, pushing the scallops toward me.

"I love seafood," I say, trying to focus on dinner. I take a few scallops and put them on my plate. "Where did you learn to cook like this?"

She shrugs. "Rebellion, mostly. Although it didn't work."

"Rebellion?"

"Yeah, my parents raised me as a vegan. When I was a teenager, I got a job working at this little lunch place up the road from where we lived. I'd never even touched meat before—I thought it was gross. But then I discovered bacon."

She smiles and pops a crumb of crisp bacon in her mouth.

"Anyway, I felt like I'd been missing all this great food, so I bought a bunch of cookbooks and spent hours watching cooking shows. Looking back, I think I just wanted attention. I thought my parents would be pissed when I started cooking all this meat, but they didn't care."

I put some asparagus and chicken on my plate. "They didn't care? If they raised you eating vegan, I'm surprised they let you sully their kitchen like that."

"Yeah, you'd think. But they just said I needed freedom to explore, so they stopped using the kitchen for themselves and let me do what I wanted."

"Wow, that's ... interesting."

"They weren't exactly conventional parents. I didn't even call them Mom and Dad. They felt they weren't respecting my energy as a human being if they lorded their position over me."

"Yeah, that's unconventional. Where do they live now? Do you see them much?"

She puts the serving fork down on the dish of asparagus. "No. I haven't seen them in a long time. They moved to Thailand the day after I turned eighteen."

"Are you serious?"

"Yeah," she says, her voice casual. "They said they'd taken me through to adulthood and now it was time for them to do what they'd been destined to do. Honestly, I think they joined some kind of spiritual group and wanted to devote their life to meditation or something."

"They just left you?"

Her face falls. "Sure. But I was an adult. They didn't owe me anything."

"Yeah, but they're your family."

"We were a weird family. They loved me in their own way, but they didn't expect to have kids. I think a doctor told my mom once that she couldn't. She was almost forty when I was born. I was really unexpected. So they kind of did what they had to do, and then went on with their lives."

I stare at her. How could her parents walk out on this beautiful, vibrant woman?

"I'm sorry, Clover. That's messed up."

"It's not that big of a deal," she says, a smile brightening her face again. "If the universe was telling them to go to Thailand, who am I to argue? I do all right on my own. And honestly, if they hadn't left, my life would be so different. I've met so many interesting people over the years, and I would have missed out on all those experiences."

But you'd have a family. My heart wants to burst for her. How much sadness is she hiding behind that brilliant smile?

"This is silly," she says, picking up the couscous. "We don't have to keep talking about me. Our food is getting cold."

My stomach growls, as if answering her, and I dig in. I take a bite of a scallop. Flavor bursts through my mouth. It's warm and tender, and savory from the bacon. "Clover, this is the best thing I've ever eaten in my life."

She positively glows. "Is it?"

I take another bite, closing my eyes. It's so good. I'm not lying to her. "Oh my god, yes. You taught yourself to cook like this?"

"Yeah." She takes a bite and looks thoughtful as she chews. "Not bad."

"Not bad? Are you kidding me? This is unreal."

I taste the other dishes, and they're just as good. The chicken is juicy, the couscous is full of flavor, and the hollandaise-drenched asparagus is amazing. I keep eating long after I'm full. I can't get enough.

While we eat, we drink wine and Clover asks about my family. I tell her about my parents, and my brothers—both my younger brother Ryan, and Hunter, who my parents essentially adopted when we were all kids. She asks about Nicole, and I tell her about Ryan's proposal at the art festival. She seems intrigued by the fact that I grew up in one little town, and returned after medical school.

Clover says she's lived all over, moving around with her parents in their RV as a kid, and then on her own as an adult. She absolutely fascinates me. Her life is like nothing I've ever heard of before—all spontaneity and whim. It doesn't seem like she plans much of anything. I have no idea what that would be like.

After dinner, we sit on the couch, finishing the bottle of wine. I love her stories about the people she's met in all the towns she's lived in. I love watching her lips while she talks. I love her smile, and her scent.

The big meal and the wine leave me relaxed, and I gradually lean closer to her, almost without realizing. Her shorts leave her legs bare and her V-neck shirt shows the tops of her breasts. Her curls brush her neck. I want to taste that sweet skin, explore that curvaceous body, feel her breath against me. My cock is so hard it's getting difficult to concentrate on what she's saying. Then the word *apartment* catches my attention.

"What was that?" I ask, suddenly feeling guilty. I was so caught up in fantasizing about her, I missed what she said.

"Oh, nothing, I just found a couple apartments that I'll call about tomorrow," she says, winding a curl around one finger. Her wineglass is perched on her bent knee. "Now that I have a job, I can focus on finding a place to live and get out of your way."

I lean back, giving her a smile I don't feel. Of course she should be apartment hunting. She's been here nearly a week, and her head is healing well. It isn't like she can stay with me forever.

"That's great. But don't feel like you need to rush. You're not in my way. Especially if you keep cooking meals like that one."

She takes a sip of wine. "Well, I figured you're newly single, right? Maybe you miss having a woman cook for you once in a while."

I laugh. "No, Jennifer didn't cook."

"Really? Never?"

"She knew how. But she never cooked for me. Especially out of the blue like this. And if she had, she would have just bitched about it getting cold when I came home late."

Clover scowls. "It's none of my business, but she doesn't sound very nice."

"You know what? She wasn't."

"How long were you together?"

"Two years."

"Why?"

The bluntness of her question makes me laugh.

"I'm sorry, I shouldn't have asked that."

"No, it's a valid question. Honestly, I don't know. When we started dating, it was a relief that she didn't care that I was a doctor. I dated a few women before her, just casually, and they only wanted me because they figured if I was a doctor, I must have a lot of money. Jennifer makes plenty of money on her own, so that had a certain appeal. But I stayed with her way too long."

"Again, why?"

I take a deep breath. "I ignored the problems. When I'm at work, I'm focused on what I'm doing, so I don't think about what's going on with my personal life. And I work a lot, so ignoring the fact that I wasn't happy with her was pretty easy. We'd fight and break up, and then she'd come back and want to work it out. Staying with her seemed easier than breaking it off."

"That's no way to live."

"No, it isn't, and it's my fault for letting it go on so long. But that's over now. And just in time too. She'd be livid if she knew you'd been staying here. I ran into her at the store last weekend and she instantly thought I was sleeping with someone."

Clover grins. "Did she? As if that's any of her business."

"That's what I told her."

"Good for you." he holds my gaze, her lips turned up in a seductive grin.

Shit.

She finishes her wine and puts her glass on the coffee table. "I kind of don't want to tell you this, but my head hurts pretty bad."

That isn't good. Concern cuts through my arousal. "You definitely overdid it today. Time to lie down."

"Yeah, I'm not even going to argue with you this time. Even though it's still early."

"No arguing."

She gets up and straightens her clothes.

I stand, putting my wine glass down. "Thanks for dinner."

"You bet. It was my pleasure."

She walks toward the stairs and I wait, rooted to the spot. Shit, I want to go up there with her. My dick is hard as fuck. But she's hurt and needs rest.

She pauses at the bottom of the stairs. "Good night, Cody."

"Good night, Clover."

I watch until she disappears up the stairs, then flop down on the couch and put a pillow over my head. I am not going to be able to sleep.

11

CLOVER

I listen to Cody shower, imagining water running down that hot body. Ever since I came downstairs that first morning, finding him in nothing but an open shirt and underwear, I can't stop thinking about it. Of course, his mother being there made things awkward, but it doesn't change the fact that he looks like a Greek god. Strong chest, muscular shoulders, washboard abs. I don't think I've ever seen a man with such a delicious set of abs in person. I want to run my tongue down them, pull out his cock, and do a better job thanking him for everything he's done for me.

Last night, I was sure things were finally going somewhere. He loved my cooking, and every girl knows the way to a man's heart is through his stomach. We sat on the couch, drinking wine, talking. I felt him moving closer to me, but then my stupid head started to hurt. A lot. Like, seeing spots in my vision, making my stomach hurt. I'm still pissed at myself for not holding out longer. I'm pretty sure he was minutes from kissing me, and that would have gone a long way toward making my head feel better.

I paused at the bottom of the staircase to say goodnight,

like I have every night since I started staying with him. I desperately wanted him to follow me up. Even though my head was killing me, I wanted him close.

Why didn't I just ask? I've never been shy about sex. My parents raised me to be free and open with my sexuality. I was taught it was normal to explore and want to experience new things. So I did. When I want sex with a man, I'm always blunt about it. I rarely wait for him to make the first move.

But Cody is different. He's so gentle and protective, but there's such a fire behind his eyes. I'm not sure what it means. He hasn't actually tried to kiss or touch me. It seems like he wants to, especially last night—but if he isn't acting on it, maybe I'm wrong. He *did* just get out of a relationship. Or maybe he just isn't attracted to me. It seems like he is, but considering I've been sleeping in his bed for almost a week and he hasn't made a move on me, I could be seeing something that isn't there.

And the truth of it is, I wouldn't be able to bear it if I'm wrong.

Being openly rejected by him is terrifying. So I hold back. I try to give him all the signs I possibly can to let him know I'm interested, but men aren't always good at picking up on those sorts of things. And if he has noticed, and isn't responding, that tells me what I need to know. I'd rather have nothing happen between us than have him tell me no.

The why of that is a mystery to me. I've never felt this way about a man. I've never been so torn between wanting someone and being scared of being rejected by him. I usually throw caution to the wind and go after what I want. I just can't with Cody, no matter how my body responds when he's near. He makes me hot and wet and almost crazy with desire. But if he didn't want me back, it would crush me.

The water turns off and I grip the covers. Maybe this will be the morning he comes in. I imagine him opening the door, peeking in to see if I'm awake. His hair would be wet and he'd be wearing nothing but a towel around his waist. I'd sit up a little and smile, nodding my head toward the bed. He'd be cautious, but I would throw off the covers, and he'd let his towel drop. His cock would be hard for me, and I wouldn't even bother undressing. I'd slide my fingers between my legs, push my panties aside and then…

I'm breathing hard and my pussy is hot. I need to stop doing that. He isn't coming in, and I'm only making it worse for myself.

I must have dozed off again because when I look at the clock it's almost nine. I'm not supposed to go to Old Town Café until tomorrow, so my day is wide open. What I need to do is find an apartment.

I go downstairs, dressed only in panties and one of Cody's t-shirts. They're so comfortable and they smell like him, so I wear them to bed every night. He hasn't said anything about it, but I'm not sure if he's noticed.

I put on hot water for coffee, grab my laptop, a jar of peanut butter, and a spoon. I'm hungry, but don't feel like making a real breakfast. I sit on the couch, and fire up my laptop.

There are already two rentals I want to call about, but I need to find more options. My credit is pretty bad, and it might be tough to convince someone to take me as a renter. I'm new in town, without a solid job history.

I dig out a spoonful of peanut butter and lick the top while I scroll through rental listings. There's a cottage that looks promising. I don't know the streets well enough to be sure of where it is. I wonder how close it is to Cody's house. It looks tiny, but the rent isn't bad.

I sigh. Usually apartment hunting is a lot of fun. New places are always so filled with possibility. But this time, they all seem drab and boring. I know it isn't the pictures. They're perfectly decent places to live. The problem is, I hate the thought of leaving.

I dip my spoon in the peanut butter again. This isn't my home. It's Cody's. And he's been perfectly sweet and chivalrous by letting me stay. I'm imposing on his hospitality. I'm well enough, I can get around on my own just fine, and I have a job. There's no reason for me to keep making this wonderful man sleep on his own couch. It's ridiculous.

The doorknob wiggles and turns. I sit up, wondering why Cody is home.

The door opens, and a woman walks in.

I know instantly it's Jennifer. She has a classic resting bitch face that would make Vivien Leigh jealous. And who else would have a key to Cody's house?

She's breaking in when she thinks no one is home. Oh, hell no.

I push the blanket off my legs so it's clear I'm only half-dressed, and mess up my curls. It takes another second for her to notice me, and her eyes widen.

She has straight brown hair with caramel highlights that are too perfect to be natural. Her makeup is very practiced—thick eyeliner and dark lips, every bit of it flawless, if a little heavy. She's wearing a beige blouse tucked into a dark pencil skirt and, I have to admit, very cute leopard-print heels.

"Excuse me," she says, walking down the short hallway. "Who the fuck are you?"

I lick my spoon. Any thoughts I had of being nice to her flee instantly. "I'm Clover. Who the fuck are you?"

"Clover?"

I smile at her as she looks me up and down, and stay relaxed, as if I totally belong here.

"Why are you here?" she asks.

"Actually, the question is, why are you here? Somehow I don't think Cody is going to be pleased to find out you're breaking into his house."

"I am not breaking in."

I roll my eyes. "Does he know you're here? Because I'll just call him and find out, if you want." I reach for my phone.

Her lips pinch together in a thin line. God, she's unpleasant looking. I can see why some men might consider her attractive—she has good features—but her awful personality ruined it within the first five seconds.

"No, you don't need to call him. I only came by to get some things I left here."

I scratch the back of my leg to call attention to the fact that they're bare. I hope she can tell I'm wearing Cody's shirt. Her eyes tighten.

This is deliciously fun.

"I'm pretty sure Cody threw your shit away."

"Listen, I don't know who you are, or why the fuck you're here, but this is none of your business."

"Actually, it's absolutely my business. You shouldn't be here. When a man leaves you, the mature thing to do is give his key back, not use it to sneak into his house when he's at work." I take another lick of peanut butter.

"He won't give a shit about you, you know," she says, crossing her arms. "You're just his attempt to get over me. But all he really cares about is his practice. Take my advice, honey. Get away while you can. Don't let him waste two years of your life."

That really pisses me off. "Maybe you just weren't the right woman for him."

"And you think you are? Hey, if you're that naïve, there's nothing I can do about it. But don't say I didn't warn you."

"Or you could have turned off the ice-cold bitch act for five minutes and at least tried to be what he needed. I don't need warnings from the spurned ex-girlfriend. I'm doing just fine, thank you very much."

She shoots me an absolutely murderous glare. Man, she hates me, through and through. Normally that would bother me deeply, but in this case the feeling is more or less mutual.

"Fine," she says, turning on her heel.

"Leave the key."

She glances over her shoulder. "Excuse me?"

"I said leave the key. There's no reason for you to have it. And it will save Cody the trouble of having one made for me."

Jennifer grinds her teeth together, twists the key off her key ring, and lets it drop to the floor at her feet. It lands on the hardwood with a clink, and her heels click as she stomps out the front door, slamming it shut behind her.

I smile and lick my spoon again. If enjoying that makes me a bad person, I'm content to call myself terrible.

12

CODY

For the first time in I can't remember how long, I leave work early. My last appointment is at four-thirty, and instead of staying for another two or three hours, I head home. Of course, it isn't some newfound sense of life balance that sends me out the front door just after five. It's my mother.

She called me this morning to remind me I agreed to bring Clover to her place for dinner. I did, didn't I? It's Thursday. I suppose it's a good thing she called, because it totally slipped my mind.

I don't think bringing Clover to dinner with my parents is a particularly good idea. My mom can be too talkative—and occasionally inappropriate. Unfortunately, Mom started the conversation by asking me whether Clover is feeling well enough to be out and about. Without thinking, I told her she is. So I can't use her injury as an excuse to put this dinner off.

As I drive home, I tell myself it will be fine. My mom is a little meddlesome, and she might ask too many personal questions, but I can handle that. Still, it feels strange to be bringing Clover to dinner with my family. She and I aren't ... well, we aren't anything. I've known her for less than a week. Despite the fact that my cock keeps trying to betray me every time I'm near her, nothing is happening between us. I can call her a friend, and be happy to do so, but she's also spent the week living in my house. Sleeping in my bed. It's so strange. Does my mom want me to bring her over because she thinks there's something going on between us? Or is she just trying to be nice to a girl who's new in town? I honestly have no idea.

I'm not sure what Clover will think about this either. She's so friendly with other people, I don't think she'll mind. At least I hope not. I don't want to spook her with this *come meet my family* thing.

I get home and find Clover pulling pans out of the cupboards. It's so odd how natural it feels to see her when I get home from work. Like she belongs here.

"Hi!" she says, giving me that glorious smile. "You're home so early. I'm not ready for you yet."

"Yeah, sorry. I should have called you, but I kind of wanted to ask you this in person."

She sets the pan down and looks at me, her blue eyes bright, her eyebrows raised. "Yeah?"

"My mom invited us to dinner at her place. Tonight."

"Oh," Clover says. "That's so nice of her."

Does she sound disappointed?

"You don't have to go if you don't want to. She mentioned it when she was here last weekend, and I completely forgot. I actually wasn't sure if she was serious. But she called me this morning to remind me. I think my brothers will be there, too, so it's kind of the whole family."

"And she wants me to come? Are you sure?"

"She's doing it for you. You know, because you're new in

town. It's what my mom does—she feeds people. It's her love language."

"I guess it's good I didn't get started on dinner." She looks down at herself. She looks adorable in a pair of pink shorts and a white t-shirt. "Do I have time to change?"

"We should leave in about half an hour. Is that enough time?"

"Yeah, I'm low maintenance." She pulls a curl and lets it bounce back. "But I must look a mess. I need to go shower."

"No, you look..." I pause. *Delicious. Sexy. Adorable. Utterly fuckable.* "Fine. You look fine."

She puts the pan back in the cupboard. "So, your ex stopped by today."

I freeze. "What?"

"Yeah, I know, it was so weird. I was sitting on the couch looking for an apartment when she unlocked the door and walked right in."

"You have got to be kidding me." A surge of adrenaline runs through my veins.

"Nope. She was surprised to see me, that's for sure. I may or may not have had a little fun with her."

"What did you do?" I ask, morbid curiosity crowding out the spike of anger.

"Not much," she says with a wicked grin. "I was in my underwear, though, so it definitely looked like I'm sleeping with you."

Oh god, it's hot as fuck hearing her say that. *Focus, Cody.* "What did she say to you?"

"That she was here to pick up her things—which she didn't do, by the way, she just left. So of course she was lying. And she told me you didn't care about me and I was just your attempt to get over her, and you'd never put me ahead of your job."

"Wow, she went straight for the throat." It isn't surprising. That was how she always felt—that my practice was more important than her.

"I kind of deserved it. She was so bitchy from the moment she walked in, I was bitchy back. I did make her leave the key, though." She picks up a house key from the counter and holds it up. "I told her it would save you the trouble of making me one."

I can't help but laugh, despite how pissed I am. I wish I'd been here to see the look on Jennifer's face when she found Clover in my house, in her underwear. I wonder if she was wearing one of my t-shirts. I've noticed she sleeps in them, which is oddly arousing—although pretty much everything about Clover is arousing.

She crouches down to put something else back in a cupboard and I watch her legs, her cute bare feet with their hot pink toenails. I want those legs wrapped around my waist.

Shit. I adjust my pants. "I'm sorry you had to deal with that. I guess now you're really wondering why I was with her."

"The thought did cross my mind. But I'd be mortified if you met some of my exes. I've dated some real dickheads. It happens."

I'm insanely curious to know what kind of men Clover dated, but I don't ask. It's the sort of thing that's tempting to find out, but probably not the best road to go down.

Clover goes upstairs to change, and I hear the shower turn on. I sit down on the couch and run my hands over my face. I'm not going up there... but holy shit, I want to.

Maybe I'm an idiot for not acting on my feelings for her, but I don't trust myself. I jumped in feet-first with Jennifer, and it was a colossal mistake. And Clover is so ... different.

She's unlike any woman I've ever met. So free and full of optimism. The woman was *this close* to sleeping in her car—with a concussion—and she was still smiling. But she also packed up and left to move to Jetty Beach on what sounded like a whim. And she said she moves around a lot, and everything she owns is out in her car.

I don't know if she's the kind of woman who sticks with something, and I'm not built for casual relationships. I never have been. If Clover isn't a woman I can envision in my future, there isn't any point in hooking up with her now, no matter how much she turns me on. I'd only be setting us both up for a lot of pain, and I don't want to do that to either of us.

I grab my phone and stare at the screen. I should call Jennifer. In the past, I often ignored it when she did something shitty. But I'm tired of being that guy. I need to deal with this before she makes things worse. I bring up her number and hit send.

Jennifer answers, her voice cold. "Cody."

"Hi, Jennifer. I suppose you know I'm calling because I heard you were at my house today."

"Yes."

I decide to be nice, but direct. "So, what was up? Did you need something?"

She's silent for a few seconds before answering. "I thought I left some things at your place."

"You should have asked. I knew you still had a key, but I'm surprised you felt like you could just come over when I'm not home."

"I just wanted my stuff." Her voice grates in my ear. "You made it pretty clear you didn't want to have anything to do with me. What else was I supposed to do? Call you? It's not like you would have taken my call."

I roll my eyes. Of course this is my fault. "You didn't even try to call. And you don't have anything here, so we both know that's bullshit."

"Yeah, your new girlfriend told me."

I sigh. "She's actually not my girlfriend."

"Oh, just a casual fuck then? I hope it makes you feel better."

"Son of a bitch, Jennifer, Clover is just a friend. She got a concussion and didn't have anywhere else to go, so I let her stay with me."

"Oh my god, she's a patient? You brought a patient home to your house? Cody, that is so unprofessional. You can't bring a patient home and start sleeping with her."

"No..." I put my hand over my eyes. Why the fuck am I discussing this with her? "That's not what's going on. It doesn't matter. I didn't call you to discuss Clover. I wanted to know why you thought it was okay to come into my house when I'm not home, but I don't know why I bothered. Of course you breaking into my house is somehow my fault, just like everything else. You left your key, but I'll change the fucking locks anyway. I don't have any of your stuff, so just back off."

"Believe me, I'm done with you," she says, and hangs up.

I toss my phone on the couch next to me. Of course she hung up. Always has to have the last word. She took zero responsibility for any of the problems in our relationship.

I can admit, I was a shitty boyfriend to her. But fuck, she's aggravating. She has a way of making herself out to be the victim every time, and it makes my blood boil.

Clover appears at the bottom of the stairs, and all thoughts of Jennifer vanish in an instant. Her hair is damp, weighing down her curls, and she's dressed in a short yellow sundress with spaghetti straps.

She comes closer and points to her hair. "I have to let it air dry, or it goes super-fro. Is this dress okay? I have no idea what to wear."

I can't stop staring at her.

"Um, is that a good look, or a bad look? I don't know you well enough to know what that expression means."

It means I want to rip that dress off of you and fuck you on this couch right now. I clear my throat. "Sorry. The dress is perfect. You look great."

"Yeah?" she asks, giving me that sweet smile.

"Definitely." I grab my phone and stand up. "You look beautiful."

"Thanks." She smooths down her dress and takes a deep breath. "Okay, let's go have dinner with your family."

"I'm ready if you are." I hold out an arm and she puts her hand in the crook of my elbow.

I'm not at all sure that I *am* ready. But she's just a friend who's new in town. I'll introduce her to my parents and my brothers. Maybe she and Nicole can be friends. That's all this is. Completely platonic.

Isn't it?

13

CLOVER

Cody's family lives in a beautiful two-story house. I can tell it's right on the beach; the sound of the waves is loud when we get out of the car. Strong wind blows my hair around my face—I'm going to look like a disaster by the time we get inside—and the salty smell of the sea is heavy in the air.

I'm beside myself with nervousness. Meeting new people is one of my favorite things, so I don't know why I'm so worried, why I'm terrified of them not liking me. People always like me. I'm friendly and good at conversation. I'm awful at plenty of other things, but meeting people and making great coffee are things I know I have a lock on.

Yet meeting Cody's family has my stomach twisted in knots. It shouldn't be such a big deal. He isn't my boyfriend, so this isn't *going to meet the boyfriend's family*. If it was, my nerves might be justified—but this is just dinner with new friends. I should be thrilled.

I feel all trembly as Cody leads me inside. The front room is so quaint, with a slightly shabby couch and a big grandfather clock. We pass a set of stairs and come into a wide-open great room at the back of the house. There's a spacious kitchen with a butcher block island, some comfy-looking seating, and a big dining table.

I recognize Cody's mother. Her graying hair is pulled back and she's wearing a long green dress. Her face breaks out in a smile when she sees me, settling a little of my nerves.

"Hi, Mrs. Jacobsen," I say.

"Please, call me Maureen. You look so much better than you did last I saw you. Cody must be taking good care of you."

My hand brushes my forehead. The lump is almost gone, although it's still bruised. "He certainly is."

Her eyes flick to Cody. "Hi, baby boy."

"Hi, Mom." He steps in to kiss her on the cheek. "Is everyone upstairs?"

"Yes, of course they are. It's such a beautiful day. Your dad is grilling something, even though I told him I'd make lasagna."

"You know Dad and his grill," Cody says.

"Oh, goodness," Maureen says, putting a hand to her chin. "I forgot to ask if there's anything you don't eat, Clover. Are you allergic to anything?"

"No, nothing like that."

"She's vegan, Mom." He winks at me.

"Oh, for heaven's sake." She opens the fridge. "Why didn't you tell me? What do vegans eat? Do you eat cheese, Clover?"

I smack Cody on the arm. "He's teasing you, I'm not vegan. I mean, I was raised that way, but I eat everything now."

She shoots Cody an annoyed look. "Well, that's a relief. Cody, get upstairs and introduce Clover to everyone."

"I will," he says with a grin. "Although she's already met everyone except Dad."

"Not under the right circumstances," Maureen says.

Cody takes me up a staircase. We emerge on the roof, but it isn't sloped. It's completely flat, with a railing going around the entire perimeter. There's seating, and patio umbrellas, and a built-in grilling station. But it's the view that makes my mouth drop open. The ocean stretches out in all its sparkling glory. A few seagulls soar through the air, and the wind blows.

"Wow. This is amazing."

"Yeah, it's pretty great. I don't ever get tired of this view."

We join the others near the grill. Cody introduces me to his dad, Ed, who's busy brushing sauce on some crackling chicken. I recognize Ryan, Nicole, and Hunter from the restaurant. Ryan looks so much like Cody, except maybe an inch shorter, with a more serious face.

Nicole is just as pretty as I remember, with shoulder-length blond hair and a friendly smile. She's wearing a turquoise dress that makes her eyes look bright blue. Hunter has a thick build, his muscular arms stretching his green t-shirt. They all ask me how I'm doing, and I assure them I'm fine.

Maureen brings up a big salad and puts it on the table, which is already set. There are bright yellow placemats, white dishes, and blue cups that look like the glass is full of bubbles. It all looks so nice and coordinated.

I swallow hard, a fresh wave of nervousness rolling through my tummy. Cody jokes with his brothers; Nicole rolls her eyes but laughs at their antics. Maureen bustles around, helping Ed bring the food to the table, and Nicole jumps in to help. I feel like I ought to pitch in, but I'm not sure what to do, and no one stops moving long enough for me to ask. My hands feel twitchy, and I have a sudden fear of dropping something. Maybe it's better if I just stay out of the way.

When everything is ready, we sit down. Maureen and Ed take the heads of the table, and the rest of us sit in between. I wind up on the end, with Maureen on my right and Cody on my left. Everyone starts grabbing food and passing it around the table. It all looks amazing, but I'm afraid my stomach is too agitated and I won't be able to eat.

"Clover," Maureen says. "Tell us about yourself. Where are you from?"

"Oh, okay," I say, glad to have an excuse to put my fork down. "Well, I lived in Walla Walla for a while. Before that, I was in Idaho. Before that…" I pause, trying to remember. "I guess it was Colorado. That was a big move. I've also lived in … let's see. Kansas for a few months, Missouri before that. Also Mississippi, North Carolina, Massachusetts, and upstate New York."

"My goodness," Maureen says. "You've certainly been all over."

"Yeah. I moved around a lot as a kid, too. We lived in an RV."

"Well, that must have been an adventurous childhood," Maureen says.

"I suppose. My parents were … different. Free spirits, I guess. They didn't like to be tied down."

"And what brought you here, to Jetty Beach?" she asks.

"Mom, let her eat," Cody says.

"It's okay," I say. "It was time for a change, I guess. People sometimes think I'm crazy, but I like to follow fate. There were signs that it was time to move on, and signs that I should come here. So I followed them."

"That's amazing," Maureen says. There isn't a hint of judgment in her voice.

The conversation turns to other things. I wonder if anyone will ask about Cody's ex, but her name doesn't come up. Ryan talks about the remodeling work he's doing on his house. Maureen and Nicole chat about the wedding. Ed asks Hunter about his business, which he says is going well. Cody asks Nicole about someone named Melissa, who turns out to be Nicole's best friend. By the look on Nicole's face, I can tell she's concerned for her friend, but they don't talk about it further, and I don't feel comfortable asking questions. Maureen starts in with stories about the three boys when they were kids, until they all beg her to stop.

I'm in awe of Cody's family. They're such normal, nice people, living in this sweet little town. They've all been here most of their lives, and seem perfectly content to stay. My nervousness doesn't dissipate as the meal goes on; it only grows. I feel like the one yellow flower in a sea of white, sticking out for all the world to stare at. They're so comfortable with each other, even Nicole. They've obviously embraced her.

I feel awful for being so fidgety, but I can't sit still. I pick at my food, trying hard to eat enough so that I won't offend anyone. It's delicious, but I'm so off kilter. I desperately want these people to like me, but I can't seem to find my usual charm. They're so ... intimidating. I know they don't mean to be, and the panic I'm feeling is entirely in my own head. Maybe it's the concussion. But I have the sinking feeling that I don't belong there, and I never will.

"Clover, will you pass the chicken down this way?" Ed asks.

"Of course." I grab the half-empty platter of chicken—

but my hands slip, and the platter crashes onto my plate, dumping the chicken into my lap.

I hesitate for a second, half-frozen with shock. The chicken is still warm, but worse is the sticky sauce dripping down my chest, beneath my dress. Cody grabs the platter, revealing my broken plate underneath. Suddenly there are hands grabbing the chicken, napkins coming from every direction, and sympathetic voices surrounding me.

I can't believe I did that.

Tears sting my eyes. "Oh, no. I'm so sorry."

I push my chair back and, clutching a napkin to my chest, hurry downstairs.

Cody is right behind me; I stop in the kitchen, trying desperately not to cry.

"Hey." He grabs some paper towels from a roll on the counter. "Here, let me help."

"No, I'm fine," I say, turning away so he can't see my face.

"Did it burn you?"

"No, it wasn't hot," I say, sniffling. "Just messy."

He's quiet, handing me a few more paper towels while I blot my dress. I get the worst of it off, but it's probably going to stain.

"Do you want to stay for dessert, or would you rather just go?" he asks, his voice quiet.

I look down at the brown smear on my clothes. I feel so stupid. I don't want to go up there and face everyone. "You can stay if you want, but I think I'd rather go."

"Okay. "Let me go up and say goodbye. I'll be right back."

I go out the front door and wait by his car, wishing I drove here myself. I don't want to have to deal with saying goodbye to everyone if they come downstairs. Of course I screwed up. It figures. I always do that when things get intense. I don't know what's wrong with me.

Cody comes out and gives me an apologetic smile. We get into the car and drive back to his place in silence. I don't know what to say. I ruined dinner with his family, and made him leave early. I really need to find a place to live so I can get out of his way. I'm only going to mess things up.

14

CODY

Clover doesn't say anything on the short drive back to my house. Glancing at her from the corner of my eye, I can tell she's fighting back tears. Dropping the platter wasn't that big of a deal. No one was hurt, and my mom certainly doesn't care about a broken plate. But it clearly bothers Clover.

My family waited on the deck while I went to check on her. My mom was perceptive enough to make sure everyone gave her some space. No one was upset about the mess, and they were genuinely disappointed when I told them we were leaving. But I wasn't going to make Clover stay.

She goes straight upstairs as soon as we get back. I toss my keys on the kitchen counter and slump down on the couch. I feel like shit. Seeing Clover upset is crushing, even if it's not my fault. The light in her eyes dims, and I want to do anything in my power to bring back her smile.

I flip on the TV and wait, listening to the faint sound of the shower. I don't pay much attention to what's on. The minutes tick by. I'm impatient for her to come down. I want to make sure she's okay, and assure her no one is mad at her. My mom texts—it's so funny that my mom learned how to text—asking how Clover's doing. I honestly don't know, but I don't want my mom to worry, so I reply saying she's fine.

Forty minutes go by, and she doesn't come down. The shower has long since turned off. Did she go to bed? Does she want to be alone?

I bounce my leg up and down, wondering what I should do—if anything. She had a mishap, and it embarrassed her. I can't blame her for that. She's been through a lot this last week. She probably needs her space. I should definitely leave her alone.

But the thought of her upstairs feeling bad, possibly even crying, is too much. I have to make her feel better.

I walk quietly up the stairs and pause outside my bedroom door. It's closed. I lift my hand to knock, but hesitate. Should I do this? She's upset and vulnerable, and maybe lying on my bed.

I'll just check on her and make sure her head doesn't hurt, maybe offer to bring her something to drink. Maybe she needs Tylenol again. I can handle that. I can control myself.

I knock softly a few times.

"Yeah?" Her voice is muffled through the door.

I open it a crack. "Hey, Clover. Can I come in?"

"Sure."

I find her sitting up on my bed, dressed in one of my white t-shirts, her hair wet. She has the comforter pulled up over her lap and she's looking at her phone.

She glances down at her clothes. "Sorry. I shouldn't wear your shirts without asking you. They're just really comfortable."

"It's okay. I don't mind."

"I am so sorry. I don't know what happened. One second I was holding that platter, and the next it was all in my lap, and dripping into my bra. I shouldn't have made you leave like that, but I was just so embarrassed."

I move closer, trying to keep my eyes from drifting down to her breasts. I can see her nipples brushing the fabric of my t-shirt. She looks adorable, all unkempt and natural. I sit down on the edge of the bed.

"You really don't need to apologize. It was an accident. They happen."

"Well, they happen to me all the time. I was so nervous, and I didn't want to screw anything up. So of course, I did."

"Why were you nervous?"

She shrugs and her breasts bounce a little. I swallow hard.

"I don't know. I guess I was worried your family wasn't going to like me. I'm so different from all of them. And you. You're all close and know things about each other. I've never had that. I don't even know what it would be like."

"You are different," I say. She looks up and meets my eyes. They're so blue and sad. "But that's what's so amazing about you. I've never known anyone quite like you before."

A tiny smile creeps across her lips. I scoot a little closer.

"Look at you. You're beautiful, and fun—and your smile? Clover, you smile and the world lights up. I can't even describe it."

Her smile grows.

So does my dick.

I'm on a roll—her expression is softening and the tears drying—so I don't stop talking. "You know how you said you remember seeing me in the restaurant, right before you hit your head? I remember that, too. I remember it because I took one look at you and I couldn't see anything else. You had this ... I don't know. This energy about you. It was magnetic. I couldn't look away. And then you got hurt, and I would have done anything to help you get better. I feel like that again, right now. I'd do anything to bring back your smile."

"Anything?" she asks, her voice almost a whisper.

My heart thunders in my chest, and my dick is hard as fuck. I want her so badly, I can hardly hold myself back. She takes deep breaths, her breasts pushing against her shirt. Her hands curl around the comforter in a tight grip, and she licks her lips.

I shouldn't. She's hurt, and I have no idea if she and I can possibly work out.

"Anything."

I brush one of her curls away from her forehead, my fingers trailing over her skin. I shouldn't have touched her. Now that I have, I can't stop. I run my hand down her face, to her neck. She's so soft. Her damp hair tickles the back of my hand. I lean in and she doesn't shy away. She moves closer, our noses touching.

I brush my lips across hers, not quite a kiss. She gasps. My hand moves around to the back of her neck and I hold her, my grip firm. Her face tilts and I surge in, feeling her mouth open for me. Her hands grasp my shirt. I slide my tongue in, savoring her sweet mouth, my body coming alive.

I want every inch of her. I hold her close, devouring her mouth. She gets to her knees and climbs in my lap, wrapping her legs around me.

She pulls away from my kiss. "It's about time."

I kiss her again and reach around to grab her ass with both hands. Oh my god, she feels so good. "Are you sure about this?"

"Oh, yes."

She pulls off my shirt and runs her hands over my chest. I lift her shirt over her head and toss it aside, then kiss her again.

Holding her ass with one hand, I cup one of her round breasts with the other. She leans her head back and moans. I run my tongue over her nipple, then put my mouth around her breast and suck. I hold her ass, and she grinds her pussy into my groin, her nipple hard against my tongue. I taste her other breast, running my tongue around her sweet skin. She rubs herself against me, her hands on the back of my neck.

"Oh my god, Cody."

I work my way back up her neck, sucking on her skin. My hands grip her hips and I lean her down so she's on her back, lying sideways across the bed. She lets her knees fall open and rubs herself through her panties with two fingers.

"You want this, baby?" she asks.

I drop my pants, kicking them away, and get on my knees in front of her. She pushes her panties to the side, revealing her soft petals of skin.

I don't want even a scrap of fabric between us. I move her hand and pull her panties off. "You're mine, now." I slide a hand up the inside of her thigh and go right for her center. I push my fingers in. She's deliciously wet, and I move in and out, feeling her body start to move. She rocks her hips, and I press my hand above her slit while my fingers work.

"Oh god, Cody, you're driving me crazy."

I lean down over her and take her breast in my mouth again, my fingers still massaging her clit. I love the way her nipple feels against my tongue. My cock rubs against her leg and she makes sweet noises with every movement of my hand. I can barely stand it.

I lift away from her and she tries to sit up. I pull my

fingers out and gently, but firmly, push her back down. "I said you're mine now."

Her mouth drops open like she's surprised, but it curls into a smile. "You take what you want then, bad boy."

"I will."

15

CLOVER

*H*oly shit, who is this commanding man, and what has he done with Cody?

I love it.

Cody runs his hands all over my body. He meant it when he said I'm his. In this moment, he owns me. He can do anything he wants.

What I want is him inside me. I'm so hot I'm dying.

He leans in and sucks my nipple, making me writhe. He grabs my wrist and guides my hand to his cock. I grip it as tight as I dare and he groans. He doesn't let go, moving my hand up and down.

"That's it, baby. Harder."

"I need this in me."

"Soon. Rub me faster."

I comply and he puts his fingers back inside me, moving with the quick rhythm of my hand around his cock.

"Oh yeah, baby, just like that," he says.

I feel wetness on my hand and I swirl it around the tip. He groans again, pushing the heel of his hand into my clit.

I'm getting close already, but I don't want to lose control. Not until he's in me.

His mouth finds its way back to mine and his tongue dives in, his lips firm but so delicious. I stroke his shaft up and down, trying to coax him to my pussy. His hand slows and I follow his lead, still keeping my fingers tight around his cock.

"No, don't stop," I say.

"Beg for me," he says with a wicked grin. He finds my clit with his thumb and rubs in a slow circle.

"Please," I whimper. How does he know how to touch me like that?

"Let me hear you. What do you want?

"I want you inside me."

He licks his lips and smiles. "I'm going to make you come so hard, Clover."

"Oh my god, Cody, do it now."

He leans over and grabs a condom from a drawer in his nightstand. In half a second, he rips open the package and slides it on.

"I'm on the pill," I say.

"It's okay, I always use one." He takes my hand and brings me up to sitting, then lays down next to me, flat on his back. "Come here." He moves me around so I'm straddling him. He grabs my hips and holds me just above him.

I run my hands down his rippling abs, rocking my hips across his tip, desperate to plunge down onto him. "Cody."

"Let me hear you."

"Cody, please."

His eyelids half-close. "That's it, baby, tell me what you want."

"I want you."

"Tell me."

"I want your cock inside me. Put it in, Cody. Give it to me."

He rams me down onto his cock and I throw my head back, shrieking with pleasure. I just had my hand around him, but I'm not prepared for how he fills me.

His hands dig into my hips. He guides me back and forth, pushing up into me each time I sink down his shaft. My pussy clenches around him, my muscles tightening.

"I want to hear you. How does that feel?"

"Oh my god, it's so good."

"Clover, you feel incredible. Oh fuck, you're going to make me come."

I grind my pussy into him. "Yeah, I am."

"Slow down, baby." He holds my hips tight, making me stop. "I don't want this to be over."

I stop moving, resting with his cock deep inside. I wanted this so badly, but I can't believe it's happening. When I went upstairs, I assumed he'd stay away, leaving me alone like he always has. I was so tempted to go to him, to find him sitting on his couch and climb into his lap, my pussy bare and ready for him. But I didn't need to. He came to me.

He slides his hands up my ribcage and cups my breasts, sliding his thumbs over my nipples. Tingles swirl through my body and I move my hips again.

"Wait," he says, caressing my breasts.

I can't refuse him. I arch my back, raising my face to the ceiling while he touches me, but keep my hips still.

"This is so hot," he says. "Look at you."

I meet his eyes and smile.

"Fuck, you're so beautiful. Your smile is everything." He reaches up and takes the back of my neck, pulling me down. He kisses me hard, one hand grabbing my ass.

I can't wait anymore. I slide up his cock and down again, grinding my clit into his groin.

He flips us over and I find myself suddenly on the bottom, his cock still inside me. He picks up the pace, thrusting in and out, his muscles rippling above me. I put my feet on his calves and buck my hips. The world seems to disappear. All I can feel is his body on mine, his cock pounding me, hitting me just right every single time.

How does he *do* that?

"Cody, I can't stop." I hold his ass and push him into me, my breath coming fast. "You feel so good."

"God, Clover, you're amazing. I love the way you feel. I could do this forever."

He runs his tongue up my breast, licking my nipple. Then he takes it in his mouth and sucks. I'm so sensitive, everything sends jolts of bliss through me.

He pounds harder, his pace quickening. I can feel how close he is. His cock swells even larger. My muscles contract, deep inside, my pussy growing hotter.

"Are you ready to come?" he asks, breathless.

"Oh, yes. Do it, Cody. Pour it into me."

He locks eyes with me, his gaze intense. He holds himself up with one arm, his other hand on my ass, guiding me. He takes me right to the edge, my climax on the brink of bursting.

"Tell me what you want." His eyes are unfocused.

"Come in me," I say, my voice barely a whimper. "Do it now."

His cock pulses and my pussy clenches around him, the orgasm saturating my being. We ride it together, calling out our pleasure in time with our thrusts. It's so intense, I don't think it will ever end.

Cody pauses, still inside me, as the last of my spasms

pass. He puts his face against my neck and kisses me while I wrap my arms around him. His weight on top of me is warm and comforting. I'm not ready to let him go.

He pulls back and looks at me, brushing my curls off my face. "That was..." He pauses, his eyes roving over me. "It was wonderful."

I caress his cheek, running my thumb along his stubbly jaw. He kisses my lips again, slow and sweet. I savor every inch of him.

He rolls off of me and takes care of the condom. We scoot around so our heads are on his pillows. He gathers me in his arms and holds me close. I lay my head on his chest and listen to his heartbeat. It nearly matches mine.

I trail my fingers up his abs. "It took you long enough."

"What?" he asks with a little laugh.

"I've been going crazy up here every night, wishing you'd just come up."

He lifts his head to look at me. "No, you haven't."

"I have. I kept the door unlocked for you."

He groans, letting his head drop back to the pillow. "I've hardly slept all week, knowing you were in my bed."

"Then why didn't you come in? I guess I didn't make it obvious enough."

"You were hurt. I wasn't going to take advantage of you like that."

I turn my face so I can kiss his chest. "You wouldn't have been taking advantage."

"Plus, we just met."

That's true, but I don't see what it has to do with anything. We're two adults who are attracted to each other —insanely attracted to each other. What's the point in denying that?

"I'm glad you came in," I say.

He lifts his head again. "Did I make you feel better?"

I smile. "Oh my god, yes. I should dump platters of chicken in my lap more often."

Cody laughs, holding me tighter.

I lay with him, enjoying the feel of his body next to mine. I think about the horoscope that sent me here. *You will be faced with important decisions that will have long lasting consequences for your life—especially your love life.* Wow, that was certainly spot on. I never imagined meeting someone like Cody, particularly the way we met.

But here I am, wrapped in his arms, floating in bliss. I try not to consider what this means, or what will happen when I find my own place. Those are problems for later. For now, I'll live in the moment, savoring this feeling.

16

CODY

I wake up Friday morning feeling more refreshed than I have in a long time. I sleep in my own bed —after last night, there's no point in sleeping on the couch —and don't bother setting my alarm. Usually I get up early and I'm the first one at the clinic.

Today, I stay in bed with Clover, her warm body pressed against me. She lets me hold her while she sleeps, which is so enjoyable. Jennifer was a light sleeper, and needed her space at night. Not that she stayed over very often. She always said she preferred her own bed to mine.

Clover snuggles against me and I relax to the soft rhythm of her breathing. Her vanilla scent fills me, and her curls tickle the bottom of my jaw. I find myself wishing I could cancel all my patients and spend the day in bed with her. She arches her back just a little, pressing her ass into my groin. My cock swells against her.

"Mm," she says. "Morning."

I slip a hand beneath her shirt and cup her perfect breast. She rotates her hips, rubbing against me. I nibble at her earlobe and she giggles.

If this is going somewhere, I need to grab a condom. I look toward my nightstand, and the time on my bedside clock catches my eye. It's nearly eight. Shit. I don't have time to do her justice.

I kiss her ear. "I'm sorry baby, I have to go to work."

She makes a sweet moaning noise in her throat and rubs her ass against me. I squeeze her breast, feeling her nipple harden. She's making it very hard to go.

"I really have to get to work." My hand runs down her belly to her hips and I push my cock against her ass.

"No. Don't go to work today."

I laugh into her hair. "I have to."

"Fuck me first. I'll make you come fast."

I groan. My cock is absolutely throbbing to be inside her. "That's not fair to you."

"I can take care of myself," she says, reaching around to grab me. She takes my cock in her hand and strokes a few times.

There's no way I can resist that. I roll to my back and reach into my nightstand, grabbing a condom. When I turn over, Clover is lying on her back, already naked, her legs open for me.

"Oh my god."

"Come here, sexy doctor man," she says. "You better hurry. You have to go to work."

I climb on top of her and plunge my cock into her hot pussy. I don't hesitate, thrusting into her, fast and hard. I lift up to my knees and grab the headboard with one hand. I want to see her.

"Tell me what to do."

Oh, fuck yes. I love being in charge during sex. It's such a turn-on.

"Use your fingers." I guide her hand down to her pussy.

"Do you want me to touch myself while you fuck me?"
"Hell, yes."
She presses two fingers above her opening.
"Fuck, Clover that's so hot."
She smiles, her fingers searching. Her mouth drops open and she moans.

I pound into her while her fingers rub her clit. Her hips rock up and down. Watching her pleasure herself while I thrust my cock in and out of her is the hottest motherfucking thing. My orgasm builds fast and her pussy contracts around me.

"Oh shit, I'm going to come all over you," she says, her voice a whimper. "Come in me, baby. Do it fast."

Her fingers rub faster and she leans her head back, her eyes closed. She's so hot, her tight pussy clamping down on my cock. I can't stand it. My cock pulses; everything goes dim. I burst into her, emptying myself, feeling the tip of my cock bottom out as I push in deeper.

Clover's fingers keep going and she calls out, her eyes closed. My orgasm ends as hers begins and I hold tight to her, keeping my cock deep inside. She contracts around me, filling me with fresh waves of pleasure.

"Wow," she says, opening her eyes. "That was short but intense."

I lean down and kiss her mouth. She opens her lips for me, her tongue eager.

"That's a good way to start my morning," I say.

She pushes against my chest and gives me a mischievous smile. "Go to work. I got what I wanted."

I laugh and kiss her again. "I see how it is. You're just using me."

"Damn straight. You keep making me come like that, and I won't give you up."

I kiss her again, then get up and get ready for work. Clover's still in bed when I finish, her legs tangled in the sheets, her eyes closed. I kiss the top of her head and she mumbles a sleepy goodbye before I head to the clinic.

Darcy is at the front desk when I walk in. She looks up, her eyebrows raised.

"Morning, Dr. J."

"Morning." I feel amazing, but I try to keep it off my face. I don't need to give the gossip patrol more fodder.

"Is everything all right?" she asks as I walk by. "You're usually in earlier."

"Yeah, I just decided to get some extra rest."

"Good for you. You work too hard."

I smile. "What time is my first patient?"

"Not until nine-thirty."

"Perfect, thank you."

I go back to my office, boot up my desktop, and open Lyle Brown's chart. His case is constantly in the back of my mind. His symptoms are so alarming. His blood work isn't back yet, but I hope it will help shed some light on what's happening. I should have ordered a more comprehensive panel when he first came to see me. I'd have more answers for him by now if I had. I skim through a few journal articles referencing muscle spasms, hoping to find something I haven't considered.

There's a knock at my door and I look up. James, my partner in the practice, stands in the open doorway.

James and I went to med school together, and he decided to move out to Jetty Beach to help me start my family practice. He has dark hair and eyes, and he's wearing a gray, striped button-down with a steel-gray tie.

"Morning, James.

"You have a minute?"

"Sure."

He adjusts his dark-rimmed glasses and comes in, shutting the door behind him. He takes a seat across my desk. "Cody," he says, then pauses. The lines in his forehead stand out and he rubs his chin. "I need to ask you about something personal."

That's odd. "Okay."

"Did you take a patient home with you last week?"

My back tightens. How does he know about Clover? "No, not exactly. She's not a patient."

James crosses his arms. "Did you treat her for a head injury?"

"I did."

"Then how is she not a patient? Because you treated her for free or something?"

"She hit her head in the restaurant where I was having dinner. So of course I helped her. What would you have done?"

"Okay, I can see that. I'm just trying to figure out how that ends with her staying at your house."

"She was new in town and didn't have anywhere else to go. With an injury like that, I couldn't very well let her sleep in her car."

James regards me through narrowed eyes for a long moment. "So you're not sleeping with her?"

Fuck. "I'm not sure what that has to do with anything."

"Son of a bitch, Cody. You're walking a very thin line here. That could be a serious ethics violation."

"Look, I did not bring home a patient. She doesn't appear anywhere in the clinic's records. I helped a woman and, yes, I gave her a place to stay."

"Did you treat her here at any point?"

"After hours and off the record."

James shakes his head. "That was a stupid thing to do. And if you're sleeping with her, it's worse. Since she's not a registered patient, it might not come back to bite us in the ass, but what were you thinking?"

"How do you know about any of this?"

He shifts in his seat. "I got a call."

"A call? Who called you?"

"Jennifer."

"Oh, for fuck's sake. You talked to my ex and now you're worried we'll get sued or something? Jennifer's just being vindictive."

"She said she came over to your house to get some things and you had a patient staying there. She said this woman answered the door in her underwear and then tried to kick her out."

"Did Jennifer tell you the part about using my key to get into my house when I wasn't here, without my knowledge?"

"No she didn't say that."

"Come on, James. You know Jen. She's pissed because I did what I should have done a year ago and finally ended it with her. Now she's trying to cause trouble."

"It's not just that. I've heard the staff talking. They said a woman came in a couple of days ago, looking for you. And that you've been acting strange."

"So now you're listening to the gossip mill? You know better than that."

"All right, fair enough. But you need to keep your problems with women out of the clinic. And if that woman who isn't a patient, who you may or may not be sleeping with—because you hedged my question—is still living at your house, I'd get her out as soon as you can. It looks bad, Cody. And sometimes that matters more than the truth does."

James gets up and leaves, sparing me the need to come up with an answer for that.

Shit. I can't believe Jennifer called him. What the fuck is her problem? She's going after my career. Clover is not a patient, and even if she was, we're both consenting adults. We haven't done anything wrong.

But James has a point. Especially in a small town, things like this can get ugly if the wrong story starts spreading. If word got out that I did something unethical—whether or not I actually did—it could have an impact on the clinic.

He's probably right. I should make sure Clover finds a place to live sooner rather than later—and keep our relationship quiet for a while.

The thought of her moving out is strangely disheartening, which is crazy. Clover can't actually live with me. I met her, what, a week ago? Jennifer and I were together for two years, and I wasn't ready to move in with her.

I imagine coming home to that sunshine smile. Clover in the kitchen, making dinner. Her shoes by the front door. Her clothes hung next to mine, her scent lingering on everything. Even before last night, it felt good to have her there. Comfortable.

Maybe too comfortable.

We're doing this all wrong. You're supposed to meet someone, date for a while, and let the relationship progress. Playing house with a girl I just met is not a healthy plan.

And it isn't like I can't still see Clover if she lives somewhere else. I certainly want to spend more time with her and see where this goes.

I tap my keyboard to turn my monitor back on and go back to the medical journals. I'll have to worry about Clover later. For now, I have patients to think about.

17

CLOVER

I roll over to the warm spot Cody left in the bed. I still feel all tingly. And a touch sore, to be honest. It's been a while since I've slept with anyone, and Cody is ... he's *ample*. I twitch at the memory of his cock inside me. Damn, he was good. Really good.

I love the way he took charge. I didn't expect that, but it was hot. I'm one hundred percent positive Ms. Resting Bitch Face didn't let him do that with her. He's probably been holding back for years. I want him to know he can unleash on me. He can be free. I want him to tell me what to do, to use my body for his pleasure. I'll just go along for the ride and enjoy every tantalizing second.

Since I'm awake, I decide to get up, despite how comfortable his bed is. But first, I bury my face in his pillow and breathe deeply. God, he smells good.

I practically skip down the stairs and go into the kitchen to make coffee. It's going to be a fantastic day. I'll go into Old Town Café and take care of the final details for my new job. Then I'll come home and make Cody something incredible for dinner. There doesn't seem to be much he doesn't like, so maybe I'll get a little adventurous with my cooking. I can get adventurous after dinner too.

I smile to myself, thinking about what he might like for dessert—and I don't mean food. What is he into? If he likes control, maybe he'll want to tie me up. I've never done it, but I could go for some bondage. Why not? I think about my hand on his dick. *That* is what I want for dessert, his big cock in my mouth.

"Woah, Clover," I say aloud. My panties are getting wet just thinking about him. "It's still morning. Let's pace ourselves."

I sit down with my coffee and read my horoscope. Nothing particularly earth-shattering, just something about being open to helping people. It doesn't really speak to me.

I hesitate, knowing what else I need to do. I should look for an apartment. In fact, I should call about the ones I already found. I can't very well keep staying here, even if the thought of leaving is pretty depressing.

I feel so comfortable here, like it's the most natural thing in the world for me to live with a man I met a week ago. That's a little bit crazy, even for me. I'm all for spontaneity and seeing where fate takes me. But whether or not Cody and I are sleeping together, I can't just shack up with him. I've never lived with a boyfriend before. In fact, it's been years since I've even had a roommate.

I sigh, trying to push away the sad feeling that blooms in my belly. I'll find something close, and we can still see each other.

After doing another quick search for rentals, I write down the most promising leads. I make a few calls. One is already rented, and another has several applications, but I'm welcome to turn one in. I decide to pass. My application isn't going to come out ahead of several others, that's for sure.

What I need is the chance to meet the owner in person, before they have a bunch of other applicants.

I'll be honest with them—there isn't any point in hiding what they'll find if they do a credit check—but I can explain my situation and hopefully convince them to take a chance on me. I've done it before. I'm not always great about paying my bills, but I do have a good rental history—although it kind of meanders around the country.

But I really like Jetty Beach. It feels different, somehow, and not just because I landed in the bed of the hottest man I've ever met. The fresh ocean air, the buzz of visitors walking down the sidewalks, the ambiance. It speaks to me. The universe definitely led me here. *Why* still remains to be seen.

I mean, there's Cody, of course—I'm sure I was destined to meet him. But maybe it's also this town. Is this finally a place to call home?

I have no idea what that would be like.

I try to ignore the deeper worry that threatens to come to the surface. I can't think about that now. I call about the little cottage I found the day before. A woman with a pleasant voice answers and says she'll be happy to show it to me if I want to come by in an hour. I feel that twitch, the one that means something. The timing is perfect. I can go look at the cottage before I go in to work. I tell her I'd love to, and say goodbye.

The cottage is literally all the things—snug and cozy, with a retro kitchen and old-fashioned lace curtains in the windows. It's furnished, which is perfect, considering I don't own any furniture. I'll need to fill it out with a few things, and get new bedding, but otherwise, it's everything I could have hoped for.

The owner is an older woman with kind eyes. I give her

my very best smile and tell her all about myself, but emphasize that I need a place to finally settle down. She doesn't seem too concerned when I admit I have some unfortunate things on my credit, and she's excited to learn I have a job at Old Town Café. She knows the owners, and says if Natalie hired me, it speaks highly of the sort of person I am.

I leave with assurances she'll call me in a day or so. I turn up the music and sing along with the radio as I drive away, heading for the café. I'm still a little sad at the thought of not staying with Cody anymore, but I have a great feeling about the cottage. I can't remember the last time I lived somewhere without shared walls. Probably when I still lived in an RV with my parents, and even then, RV parks aren't usually quiet places. I bet the little cottage is peaceful at night.

I pull up to a stop sign. There aren't any other cars around. The main streets in town get downright crowded, but I've hardly seen any other traffic on the back roads. I press on the gas and my car sputters, then jerks forward, bouncing me in my seat. The engine makes a weird grinding noise and dies.

Oh no.

I turn the key and try to start it again. Nothing. I pat the steering wheel, as if I can coax my car back to life.

"Come on, baby, don't fail me now." I turn the key again.

The engine revs, but won't turn over.

I look at the clock. I'm supposed to be at the café in twenty minutes. Can I walk there fast enough? I'm not sure, but I can try. There's no way I'm going to call Natalie and tell her I'll be late. Talk about a horrible start to a new job.

I get my phone, hesitating. Cody is at work, and I know he doesn't want to be bothered during the day. And he's already rescued me so many times, I'm beginning to lose track of all the ways I owe him.

But I don't know anyone else in town well enough to have their number.

I look up at the street sign to see where I am and send Cody a text. *I am so sorry to bother you, but my car died at the intersection of Anchor Street and Starfish Lane. I have to be at the café in 20, so I'm going to walk, but my car is in the middle of the road. Don't know who else to call.*

I set the emergency lights flashing and take my purse. It feels weird to leave my car sitting there, but there isn't much I can do if it won't start. I certainly can't push it out of the road, and I know nothing about cars.

I could pop the hood and stare at it for a while, hoping for some nice person to drive by and help me, but then I'll definitely be late for the café.

My car will probably be towed before I can find a way to get back to it, but I guess it needs a tow anyway. Thing is, I don't know how I'll pay for a car repair. I sigh and close the door, locking it behind me. Jetty Beach is small enough, I can live without a car. Although the cottage I just saw won't work. It's too far from town. That's disappointing. It seemed so perfect.

I take a deep breath and start walking toward town.

My phone dings with Cody's text. *Stay where you are. Rescue incoming.*

God, he is so sweet. I answer. *It's okay. I think I can make it if I walk.*

I continue up the road. At least I'm wearing decent shoes. And the sun is shining, so that's a plus. This would have been worse in the rain.

But I haven't gone far when the rumble of an engine

comes from behind me and tires crunch on the gravel as a truck pulls over.

"Hey," someone says behind me. "I hear you need a ride."

I turn to see Cody's brother, Hunter, leaning out of the driver's side window of a green Toyota pickup.

"Hey. Um, yeah, my car died back there."

"I passed it. Come on, get in."

I climb in the passenger's seat. "Thank you so much. How did you get here so fast?"

"I live close. "Cody texted and said you had car trouble, and I'm off work today."

I stare at him, not sure what to say. Cody texts him saying the perfect stranger who walked out on his family dinner after breaking a plate and spilling chicken all over herself needs help and this guy just ... gets in his truck and picks her up?

"Oh, and don't worry about your car." He pulls back onto the street and heads toward town. "Ryan's on his way. Between the two of us, I figure we'll get it started and at least take it back to Cody's place for you. Can I have the keys?"

Wordlessly, I hand him my keys.

"Perfect. Car troubles are the worst, aren't they?"

His other brother is coming, too? For me?

"You'll probably still need to take it in to an actual mechanic," Hunter continues. "I know enough to hopefully get it running, but you'll want a pro to take a look so you don't have this problem again. I know a guy in town. He's a good guy—won't screw you over or anything."

A lump rises in my throat. I want to thank him again—not like I can ever thank him enough—but I can't get a word out. I don't want to cry.

Hunter's phone saves me the trouble. "Hi, Mom. Yeah, I

picked her up. Oh, she's fine. No, she has to go to work. I'm not sure about after, but I'll ask her. Pie sounds great, you don't have to tell me twice."

He pauses and is silent for a moment.

I glance at him from the corner of my eye.

He takes a deep breath, and his brow furrows. "No, I haven't. Look, Mom, I don't really want to talk about that right now. Okay. Love you, too. Yes, I will text you when I drop her off so you know she got to work safe, even though that's going to be in like ninety seconds. Okay, Mom. Bye."

I swallow hard and find my voice. "Did your mom just call about me?"

"Yeah, word travels fast with the Jacobsens," he says with a chuckle. "Cody texted me, because he knew I was close, and I gave Ryan a call, since I figured I could use help with your car. Who knows how Mom found out. She probably called Ryan and he told her. Oh, and she invited you over for pie tonight."

"Pie?" I say, my voice weak.

"Yeah, she makes the best pie you'll ever eat." He pauses, glancing at me. "Don't feel obligated though. She'll understand if you can't come. You've had a stressful day already."

I stare out the window as he drives into town. I make friends wherever I go, but I'm never very close to any of them. I don't even have many contacts in my phone. I see people when I see them, like Mrs. Berryshire when she would sit outside her front door. But that's it. I date when I meet someone I'm attracted to, and I'm usually friendly with the people I work with. Outside of that, I take care of myself. That isn't always easy, but it's the only way I know how to live.

This entire family stopped what they were doing to help me and I can't fathom why. As far as they know, I'm just a charity case Cody picked up. No one knows what happened between Cody and me last night. At least, I don't think they know. I'm no one to them—just some random girl.

Hunter pulls into a parking spot down the street from the café. "What time do you get off work?"

"I'm not sure. I don't officially start until tomorrow, so I'm just here to fill out paperwork and stuff."

"Okay." He grabs his phone and types out a text. "I'll just let Ryan know to meet me here, then. I'll come in and get some coffee and a sandwich or something. I'm hungry anyway. If you'll be longer than, say, an hour, Ryan and I can go check out your car. But if you won't be long, we'll just wait."

My chest constricts and the lump in my throat rises again. My phone dings with a text from Cody.

Hey sunshine, did Hunter find you?

I reply. *Yes. We're at the café. About to go in.*

Good. I was worried. I can't leave here until later, but we'll make sure you have a ride home. I'll see you tonight.

I bite the inside of my cheek to keep tears from welling up in my eyes. I have to pull myself together before I go in.

Hunter smiles at me. "Okay, we're all set. Let's go get you started at your new job." His voice is downright cheerful.

I take a shaky breath, pushing down my swelling emotions. "Thank you so much for all of this."

He shrugs. "Sure, it's no problem. We'll get you all taken care of. Don't worry."

I *am* worried. Not about my car, or my new job. I'm worried about the feeling in the pit of my stomach. I'm so grateful to Cody and his family, but it scares me. I don't know how I'll ever repay these people. I don't know how to thank them.

I don't want to screw this up.

18

CLOVER

My orientation at work goes well. Natalie is just as pleasant as she was the first time we met. The café is pretty standard. I'm not supposed to be working, officially, but I jump in and make coffee when a line forms at the front counter. Hunter has lunch while he waits for me, and Ryan joins him.

Natalie shows me around and introduces me to Harold, one of the cooks. I fill out the employment forms, then she sends me on my way with my schedule for the coming week. It isn't quite full-time hours, but she says she'll be able to work me up to it. She has me working early mornings, which suits me well. I like being done with my workday in the early afternoon, so I have my evenings to myself.

Hunter drops me off at Cody's, insisting he and Ryan will handle my car. I hate the idea of them spending their free time dealing with my problem, but they're so easygoing about it—and they don't listen to my arguments, taking me to Cody's place despite my protests. There isn't much I can do.

A couple hours later, they pull my car into Cody's driveway. Hunter's face is triumphant when he tells me he fixed the problem. He won't even let me pay for the part he bought, telling me with a wink that I can just give him my employee discount when he comes into the café.

My plan to cook Cody dinner went down the drain, but he brings takeout and we curl up on the couch together with dinner and a movie. My head is still reeling from everything his family did for me, but he acts like it's nothing. I'm filled with gratitude, but I hate feeling indebted to them—and to Cody.

I have to work early the next morning, but Cody's still worried about my car, so he gets up and drives me. Natalie shows me the opening routine. The first several hours go by in a blur as I help her prep the shop, then wait on customers when we open.

I take a break about halfway through my shift, and check my messages. I have a voicemail about the cottage. She's happy to rent it to me, and since it's vacant I can move in anytime.

I'm so relieved. I don't want to keep depending on Cody for everything. It isn't like me.

Cody picks me up from work. The news bursts from my lips as soon as I sit down in his passenger's seat.

"I found a place to live."

"Already? Wow, that's ... obviously, that's great."

"I know. It's completely perfect. It isn't even an apartment, it's this cute little cottage, and it already has furniture. Even if I don't get full-time hours at the café, I won't have any trouble affording it."

Cody pulls out onto the street and turns toward his house. "Great news."

"Isn't it?"

But something about his voice tells me Cody isn't so sure it's *great*, despite having used that word twice.

"Aw, are you going to miss me?" I mean it as a playful tease, but when he looks at me his eyes are intense.

"Yes, I am."

I don't know what to say to that, so we spend the rest of the drive back in silence.

My car seems to be running fine, so I drive over to my new place the next day. Cody helps me bring in my stuff—it's not like there's a lot of it. Moving is pretty easy when you barely own anything. Cody's mom comes by with groceries. I thank her profusely, trying to hide my bewilderment. Are these people for real?

Cody stays for a while, but eventually says he should get home. We both have to work early the next morning. He kisses me goodbye, his mouth lingering against mine as he stands in the doorway. I think about asking him to stay, but it seems like it's time for me to be on my own again.

I shut the door behind him and lean against it, breathing out a long breath. This is good. My new place is adorable. It has a little kitchen at the back that's open to the rest of the house, with a small dining table that separates it from the living room. There's a wood fireplace—I've never had a fireplace in my life—and a comfortable couch next to an oversize chair. I don't have a TV, but I can watch stuff on my laptop, and the room doesn't have much space for anything else. Down a small hallway are two bedrooms, and a bathroom with pink tile.

I haul the new bedding I bought down to one of the bedrooms and make the bed. When I finish, I stand back and look at my handiwork. The comforter is light gray with a white paisley pattern—a nice balance of soothing and girly. It's a lovely bedroom. I'll be very happy here.

I take a shower and shave my legs. There's nothing quite like new sheets against freshly shaved legs. I open the dresser, looking for a tank top to wear to bed—and the drawer is full of Cody's t-shirts.

Oh my god.

He must have put them there when I was busy bringing stuff in from my car. I grab one and hold it to my nose, breathing him in. I slip it on and climb into bed.

I lie there for a long while, unable to sleep. It's eerily quiet. Crickets and frogs sing their evening songs outside my window, but no cars drive by. No sounds of neighbors stomping, or fighting, or having sex carry through the walls.

It's going to take some time to get used to this.

After a while, I groan and turn over. I'm bored. My body is tired from working, but my mind won't relax.

And I miss Cody.

God, that's stupid. Nine days, I've known him. Not even two weeks. Usually my first night in a new place is filled with excitement, but I'm not awake because I'm thrilled with my new digs. I've only had a taste of Cody, and I want more. My body wants more.

I think about his strong chest, his muscular arms, those ridiculous abs, his adorable dimples. The way he takes what he wants, tells me what to do. My hand slides down my belly, beneath my panties, and I press my fingers against my clit. I let my eyes flutter closed as I swirl my fingers around and imagine Cody's swollen cock, plunging in, stretching me. He feels so good. I haven't slept with every guy I've dated, but I've been with my share, and no one has ever filled me the way Cody does.

I pull my hand away, frustrated. Buttering my own muffin is not going to cut it tonight. I'm keyed up, but I don't just need a quick release. I need Cody.

I glance at the clock on my phone, wondering if he's still awake. It's just before eleven, but we both have to get up early. I definitely shouldn't wake him. It would be silly to get up.

I just moved into my new place, I should at least spend the first night in my own bed.

Maybe I'll just text him.

Hey, are you still awake?

His reply comes only seconds later. *Yes, is everything okay?*

I smile and lick my lips. *I'm fine. Miss you.*

Baby, I miss you too.

I sigh. This is so crazy. But fuck it.

I get up and throw on a pair of leggings and a sweatshirt. I get my purse and keys and open the front door. The cold night air hits me, raising goosebumps on my arms. I stop. I shouldn't do this. It's not like we aren't going to see each other soon. I can hang out with him tomorrow. I can certainly wait a day.

I glance down at my keys and draw my eyebrows together. There's my new house key, and the big black key to my car. But there's a third key there. One I didn't put on my keychain.

It's Cody's.

He put his house key on my keychain. I smile and hurry out the door. If that isn't fate telling me to go to him, I don't know what is.

I pull up to his house, my heart racing. His last text came mere minutes ago. My cottage is less than a mile from his house, and it took no time to get here. I creep up to the door, feeling like a kid sneaking around, and slide the key into the lock. It turns, and I go inside.

The lights are off. I take off my shoes and walk up the

stairs, taking quiet steps. A sliver of light filters onto the landing from his bedroom. I lean close to the door, putting my mouth near the edge.

"Cody?"

The floor creaks and the door opens.

His mouth is on mine, his hands pulling off my clothes. I stumble in, dropping my purse to the floor, yanking off my sweatshirt. Cody's hands are firm, dragging my leggings off. He rips off his shirt, kissing me again as soon as the fabric goes over his head.

He leads me into his room, his mouth never leaving mine, until his legs hit the bed. I break the kiss and work my way down his neck, to his chest. I run my tongue down the ripples of his abs, my hands on his hips.

I wrap my hand around his thick cock and take the tip into my mouth. Cody groans, running his hands through my hair. I move my tongue around, sliding it across his swollen flesh. I open wider, pulling in the crown, and suck hard.

Cody shudders. "Holy shit."

I stroke up and down with my hand while I suck on the top, drawing as much into my mouth as I can take. Cody's hands on my head are gentle, guiding me up and down. I raise my gaze to look up at him. He meets my eyes and he moans again. I smile at him, curling my lips around his cock.

"You have got to be kidding me," he says, breathing hard. "You are the hottest woman on the fucking planet."

I move faster, stroking him with a firm grip, plunging him into my mouth. His eyes close and he leans his head back.

His dick pulses, and I can tell he's close. I'd let him come in my mouth if he wants to, but he touches his fingers to my chin and draws me up.

"Come here."

I stand and he nudges me onto the bed. He grabs my hips and pulls me so my ass is right at the edge. His teeth graze my inner thighs and I shiver.

"Mm, I want to taste you."

I'm throbbing for him, my pussy positively aching. He works his way up with his tongue and his teeth, nipping at my skin, driving me insane. His tongue reaches my center, and he finds my clit almost instantly.

I moan. "Holy shit, Cody, you make me crazy."

His tongue works up and down, literally making my toes curl. I grab the sheets and move my hips with his rhythm, panting as he devours me. He sucks on my clit and I shriek. It feels so fucking good.

He stops with a suddenness that takes my breath away. I lift my head and he grins at me, his dimples showing beneath his stubble.

"What do you want, baby?"

"I want that cock in me."

"I want to hear you beg," he says, still smiling.

"Please," I say, my voice breathy.

He pulls my hips slightly off the bed, his hands holding my ass, and presses his cock close. He reaches over, grabs a condom, and slips it on.

"Tell me again."

"Please, baby."

"I love it when you beg."

"Take me," I say, meeting his eyes. "You can have all of me."

He pushes his cock in, and I moan loudly. Standing beside the bed, his hands on my hips, he pounds me hard. I wrap my legs around him and let him set the pace. It doesn't matter what he does. Short of him pulling out and walking away, I'm coming. Soon.

"God, Cody, you're so good."

He keeps thrusting, every move bringing me closer to the edge. He's thick and hot and powerful. I love seeing his cock move in and out of me, the cuts of his sleek muscles rippling as he fucks me. He's so damn sexy.

He stops, holding tight against me, his cock deep inside. His chest moves fast with his breath, his abs tight.

"Turn over."

He pulls out and I'm quick to obey. I get on my knees and look back at him over my shoulder.

He climbs up on the bed behind me and grabs my hips, sliding his cock in. "Keep your hips up, but put your chest down."

I bend at the waist, lowering my upper body to the bed, and keep my ass in the air. He pulls halfway out and pushes in again. Oh my god, this angle. He thrusts in and out, and it's like magic.

"Fuck, yes," I say, panting.

"Do you want it harder?"

"As hard as you want. Fuck, Cody, this is good."

"God, Clover, I love the way you feel," he says between thrusts. "You're perfect."

He pounds me harder, and my thoughts flee. I can't think of anything but this man and his cock moving in and out of me. He works me into a frenzy, my body on fire.

His cock pulses and I let out a low moan.

"Make me come." I'm desperate, aching for release, every thrust driving me crazy. "Please, baby."

Cody pulls out and I gasp. He flips me onto my back and wastes no time climbing on top of me and plunging in again.

"I want to see your face. You're so fucking beautiful."

He leans down and kisses me, his mouth hungry. I open for him, parting my lips, widening my legs.

He quickens his pace, fucking me with fury. I'm flying, every move he makes sending me higher.

"Are you ready for this, baby?" His breath comes fast and his chest glistens. "I want you to come with me."

"So ready."

He speeds up and the tension builds, my core muscles contracting. I feel my climax building, growing from deep inside. It's like an orgasm on another level, something I've never felt before.

"Don't stop." My eyes flutter closed, my mouth open. It's so good, I can barely stand it.

Cody keeps going, then slows down, burying his cock deep into me. He bottoms out with every stroke, sending shockwaves of pleasure through my whole body.

"Are you ready for this?"

"Do it."

He explodes inside me, his cock throbbing. Each pulse is a jolt of electricity, lighting me up. I come in a rush, the pleasure so intense I almost can't breathe. It goes on and on, like it will never end, wave after wave rolling through my body. I cry out, holding nothing back, gripping the sheets as he pours into me.

The shockwaves subside and Cody looks down at me. We're both breathing hard. He leans down and kisses my neck, moves up to my mouth. I wrap my arms around his neck, reveling in the feel of his mouth on my skin, his tongue brushing my lips.

"I'm glad you're here," he says softly.

I lean my head back to look at him and smile. "Me too."

19

CODY

Clover does eventually sleep at her place—with me, usually. We settle into a routine of seeing each other most nights after work. It's rare that we sleep apart, instead crashing together at my place or hers.

Sometimes she lets herself into my house before I get home, and makes dinner. I love coming home and seeing her car in my driveway. I walk in the door and she's there, that brilliant smile lighting up the room. She rushes into my arms and I kiss her mouth, her cheeks, her neck. I pick her up, grabbing her tight ass, and she wraps her legs around my waist. Sometimes we stop and have dinner. Other times we're too busy tearing our clothes off and fucking wherever we end up. It doesn't matter. Food can always be reheated.

Weeks go by; the summer cools into fall. The tourists fade away, only filling the town on weekends. Clover's job seems to be going well. I stop by often, grabbing lunch at the café when I know she's working. Customers get to know her, and she learns the names and favorite drinks of all the regulars. Despite her worries about being clumsy, she never seems to have any trouble. People love her.

After a while, I stop keeping my relationship with Clover a secret at work. There are a few days of whispered conversations among my staff before it quiets down—or at least the whispers are all behind my back so I no longer hear them. James even asks how we're doing, so I figure he's not as concerned about how it might look. I find myself working less than usual—going in later, and leaving earlier in the evening. It makes it harder to keep up with everything, but I'm enjoying my time with Clover so much I try not to worry about it.

I'm still struggling to figure out what's going on with Lyle Brown. His blood work comes back, but I don't find anything conclusive. I rule out several worrisome possibilities, but I'm not any closer to a definitive answer. I have my nurse call him to schedule more tests. I hope we can find a clue as to what's happening to him.

I close Lyle's chart and open my email. I have that medical conference coming up, and there's an email with the agenda. Truth be told, most of it looks pretty dull, but there are a few sessions I'm interested in. Clover's coming with me, so I decide to search for some restaurant possibilities. It's in Portland, and there are a lot of great choices. I want to take her somewhere nice.

My phone dings with a text from her. *Hey sexy. Do you still have patients?*

I can't help but smile. I open my calendar and check my schedule. It's four o'clock, and my last patient was at three. It's unusual, but it's also Friday, and I can't say that I mind.

No more patients today. Are you off work?

Her reply is almost instantaneous. *Come outside.*

Wondering what she's up to, I head out to the parking lot.

I'm greeted by the rumble of a very loud engine. I don't

see Clover's car anywhere. The engine revs a few times and a motorcycle pulls up to the curb. The driver takes off her helmet, releasing a mass of blond curls.

Clover smiles, looking positively giddy as she turns off the engine.

"What the hell is this?"

"I borrowed it from a friend at work." She puts the helmet down and clasps her hands together. "I have the best idea."

"I hope it involves someone else picking up this death-trap and you driving home with me."

Clover swings her leg over the side and gets down. "No, we're going on a road trip."

"On that? No."

"Yes! Right now. Let's just take off."

"What are you talking about? I can't just leave."

"You said you don't have any more patients. But I actually knew that already because I called Darcy at the front desk before I texted you. She said you're free for the rest of the afternoon."

I want to be annoyed that she called Darcy to ask about my schedule, but it's actually pretty sweet. But a motorcycle? "Clover, do you know what happens to someone in a collision on one of those things? It's bad. You don't walk away from that."

"I have helmets. Come on, Cody. You have to take risks sometimes."

I rub my chin. "This is crazy. Where do you want to go?"

"I'm not telling." She bites her lower lip as she smiles at me, and bounces up onto her toes.

"Clover..." I'm trying to think of a good reason not to do this, but I'm not coming up with anything.

"Come on. The weather is supposed to be dry for the

next week at least. There's no reason you can't leave work. I'm off until Monday. Let's do this. It will be so fun. I've always wanted to go on a road trip on a motorcycle."

"Do you even know how to drive that thing?"

"Of course I do," she says, like she can't believe I'd even ask.

I cross my arms. Part of me hates this idea. Motorcycles are dangerous as shit. I went through a phase during med school where I drove one, but after treating my first motorcycle crash victim during my residency, I sold it.

But Clover gets on and arches her back. The way she looks straddling the seat is too hot for words.

"Come on, baby," she says. "You know you want to. I'll even let you drive."

I glance over at my car. "How about I meet you back at my place and I'll think about it? If we take off, I need to grab some stuff from home anyway."

"Nope," she says, and licks her lips. "I already packed everything we'll need. Let's go. Now."

My back is tense, but she curls a finger, beckoning me closer. Her lips part in a dazzling smile.

"You know you want to. I promise, you're going to be glad you did."

I groan and step off the curb.

Clover squeals and gets off the bike, then pulls me in for a kiss. She takes off my tie and unbuttons the top two buttons on my shirt. She stows my tie in a bag she has strapped to the back, and produces my sunglasses and a casual jacket. She slides the glasses on my face and messes up my hair.

"There," she says, adjusting my open collar. "So hot." She hands me a helmet and I put it on. She dons sunglasses and the other helmet, and we both climb on the bike.

Clover wraps her arms around me. It's been a while, but driving it is like ... well, like riding a bike. It all comes back to me in seconds. I take it easy as we drive through town, but when we get to the highway, I open it up a little. The wind rushes past, the engine purrs beneath me, and Clover holds me tight.

I don't want to admit it, but it's kind of fucking awesome.

We stop at a random hotel for the night, and Clover still doesn't tell me where we're going. Taking off with no plans is so far outside my comfort zone, but with Clover it's more exciting than stressful. The hotel sucks, but it only makes us laugh. In the morning, we get up early and continue on our drive. Clover consults her phone and tells me to keep heading east across the mountain pass.

On the east side of the mountains, we stop for lunch at a little roadside café. The waitress brings us club sandwiches.

"So, are you going to tell me yet?" I ask.

She bounces in her seat, pursing her lips, her eyes sparkling. "Okay, fine. We're going to the Gorge."

The Gorge Amphitheater is an incredible outdoor concert venue. I haven't been to a concert there in years. "What's going on at the Gorge?"

She smiles again, looking like she might burst. "I got us tickets to see Sweet Water."

My mouth drops open. It's a Seattle band I was into years ago. How does she even know that? I might have mentioned it once, but I'm stunned she remembers. "Sweet Water? I didn't even know they were still around."

"I know. I heard about a month ago that they got back together and are playing the Gorge. You told me once that you used to be into their music. You said you wished you could see them play live again, because they were really good and you had such a great time at their last concert. So when I heard about this, I bought us tickets. It's been so hard to keep it from you."

Her thoughtfulness disarms me. One little conversation, and it sparks this crazy road trip. All for me.

"Clover, you're amazing."

She smiles brighter and I lean across the table to kiss her.

The concert is fantastic. They play a mix of the old songs I remember and new stuff that's really good. We have a few beers, and I get a little buzzed from all the people smoking weed around us. Clover is fucking adorable, jumping to the music and screaming with the crowd.

It's late when we finally find a hotel room after the concert. The next morning, we get back on the road. The weather is great, if a little cold with the wind rushing by, and we fly down the freeway. Despite my initial hesitance, I'm more relaxed than I've been in months. Or maybe years.

Turns out, it feels great to throw caution to the wind and do something unexpected. I'm a guy who tends to do things by the book, but I like how Clover's making me see the world in a new way. I never would have bothered getting concert tickets for a venue five hours away, let alone turning it into a road trip on a motorcycle. But this is just what I needed.

Maybe Clover is, too.

20

CLOVER

The last few months have been completely fantastic. Since taking Cody to the concert, I've come up with more ways to surprise him, although nothing quite as crazy as borrowing a motorcycle for a road trip. He won't admit it, but I know he had fun driving it. He looked hot as hell, too. His responsible doctor look is super sexy—he's always so put together with his adorable button-down shirts and ties—but messing him up a little was fun, too. I like to keep him on his toes.

One Wednesday, I convince him to leave work early so we can go to a movie, but I insist on sitting in the back so we can make out like teenagers. About a month later, I let myself into his house before he gets off work. When he comes home, I greet him from his dining table, wearing nothing but a few dollops of whipped cream and a well-placed cherry.

That's definitely one I'll do again.

Another night, we have a few drinks and I convince him to break into his neighbor's backyard while they're on vacation so we can sit in their hot tub. The risk of getting caught is thrilling as hell, and we have some amazing sex. He wakes up the next morning worried they might have a surveillance camera.

Early one November morning, I head to work. It's still dark, and the clear sky is peppered with stars. Natalie isn't in the café when I get there. That's unusual. The crowds have thinned out even on weekends, but she's still usually here before me, baking the day's batch of muffins. Instead, the whole place is empty. It's a Thursday, so I know it won't be too busy, but we always have fresh baked goods.

I text Natalie to see if everything is okay, and wait about five minutes for her to answer. I don't get a response. I stand near the front counter, eyeing the kitchen. I don't have a lot of time before I have to turn on the open sign, but it's enough to get a batch of muffins in the oven. I've never baked for the café before—and for all I know Natalie is bringing something from her kitchen at home—but I decide not to take a chance.

I find all the ingredients in the back, and whip up the muffin batter. I get the first batch in the oven and have to open the café. My early morning customers wander in and I get them coffee, chit-chatting with them like I always do.

The muffins come out, and I stock the case. Still no word from Natalie. There aren't many customers, so I'm doing fine on my own, but I'm worried that something is wrong. I duck into the kitchen for a moment and call her.

"Clover, I'm so sorry," she says as soon as she answers. "My father had to go to the hospital in the middle of the night and I'm still here. I lost track of time. Are you at the café?"

"Yeah, I'm here. I baked some muffins. I hope that's okay."

Natalie makes a little noise. I think she might be crying.

"Thank you so much. Yes, that's more than okay. I'm so sorry you're there on your own. Harold can't be there until ten. Can you handle everything until then?"

To be honest, I'm not sure if I can handle everything for three hours, but Natalie sounds like she's falling apart. I'll just have to deal. "Yes," I say, trying to sound confident. "I can handle it until Harold gets here."

"I owe you for this. You can tell people we don't have breakfast today because there's no cook. It's just one day, and it shouldn't be too busy."

"Don't worry, Natalie. I've got this."

I hang up, blow out a breath ... and realize I feel the tingle. *Fate.* It's trying to tell me something, but I'm not sure what.

I don't have time to ponder. A few more customers come in, wanting coffee, and I sell some of the muffins. They're still warm, and I even get a nice compliment. It's slow enough that I prep some things for breakfasts, in case anyone orders something. My hands are a little jittery, but luckily I don't drop anything.

Just after nine, a man comes up to the counter. I've seen him before, but he's not one of my regulars. He's tall and quite nice-looking, probably in his early thirties, with short, dark blond hair and clear blue eyes.

"Morning," I say.

He takes a menu and glances at the choices. "What do you recommend for breakfast?"

"Well, we're a little short on staff this morning. But it's slow right now, so I can whip something up for you."

"Yeah? What's your specialty?"

"To be honest, I'm better at dinners than breakfasts, but I do make a pretty mean omelet."

"All right, an omelet, then."

"What kind?"

He shrugs his shoulders and puts down the menu. "Surprise me."

I smile and ring him up, then head back to the kitchen.

It isn't on our menu, but I immediately grab some smoked salmon. We get it locally, and it has such great flavor, I just know it will make a wonderful omelet. I bustle around the kitchen, checking a few times to make sure I don't have any customers at the counter. I add the salmon to the eggs with a few bits of cream cheese. I sprinkle green onions over the top and garnish the plate. It smells heavenly. Hoping I haven't made a huge mistake, I bring it out and serve it to the customer.

He thanks me, and a few more people come in. I have to run back to the kitchen to make a couple breakfast sandwiches, and we're almost out of muffins but I don't think I have time to make more. I put on a fresh pot of coffee and Mr. Nice Looking Omelet Guy comes back to the counter.

"Hey," I say, brushing a curl back from my forehead. "I'm sorry, do you need more coffee?"

"No, I'm fine. Is that omelet on your menu?"

Uh oh. "No, it's not. You said surprise me, and I just had this feeling I should use the smoked salmon. I'm so sorry. Was it awful? I can make you another one."

"No, it was amazing. How often do you make those? Is it a special of the day or something?"

"Well ... never, actually. I'm not the cook. I'm just trying to keep us afloat until the real cook gets here. I've never made that before."

"So you made that up, just now? Where did you go to culinary school?"

I probably shouldn't laugh, but I do. "Nowhere."

"Then where did you learn to cook like that?"

"Honestly? Food Network. And YouTube."

He looks at me for a moment, a half-smile on his face. "That's impressive. What's your name?"

"Clover Fields. And yes, it's my real name."

"I'm Gabriel Parker," he says, and I take his hand to shake it. "That was one of the best things I've eaten in a long time. If you threw that together just now, your instincts are very good."

"Wow, thank you."

"I don't know if you'd be interested, but I'm the head chef up at the Ocean Mark. I've been looking for a new sous chef. Maybe you could stop by and we could chat?"

My mouth drops open and it takes me a second to recover. "You're joking, right?"

"Not in the least. You don't have formal training, so we'd have to talk about what you know how to do, but you were spot-on with this. I'd love to see what else you can do."

I stare at him. He must be kidding. A sous chef? But I feel the tingle. "I—um—" I stammer, not sure what to say. "I'm sorry, I wasn't expecting this. But yes, I'd love to."

"Great." He slides a business card across the counter. "Give me a call and we'll set something up."

I take the card, ready to jump out of my skin. This is huge. I like working at the café, but a sous chef is, like, a career. I've never had that before. I've always worked to pay my bills, because that's what you do. But I've never worked toward something bigger.

I've never stayed in one place long enough.

I get through the rest of my shift, torn between excitement and fear. I can't wait to tell Cody, but thinking about a career brings up all sorts of feelings I'm not sure about. It sounds permanent. Like staying.

That's what I want, isn't it? What I've been searching for?

I've been following fate, listening to the signs the universe sends me. I wound up here, and for all I can tell it was totally meant to be.

Then why does that scare me?

My hands are jittery as I drive home. I planned to make dinner for Cody and me tonight, so I change clothes and get some groceries at the store. Cody's kitchen is bigger than mine, so I send him a quick text to let him know I'll meet him at his place after he gets off work. He doesn't reply, but I don't worry about that. He's probably busy with patients.

Cooking usually relaxes me, but I find myself getting more tense as I work. A phone call from Cody's mom doesn't help. She asks if he and I can make it to dinner on Sunday, and I realize we've been having dinner there almost every Sunday for months.

I sauté some chicken in white wine sauce and make butternut squash with a butter cinnamon glaze. It smells like fall. That should make me happy—I love fall—but I'm tempted to throw it all away. What am I doing in Cody's house, cooking him dinner in his kitchen, like I'm some kind of housewife?

When was the last time I went a day without seeing him? Weeks ago? And then it was only a day. This isn't like me. I'm always on my own. Even when I've dated men in the past, I never spent this much time with them.

I knew Cody for all of a week and a half before I had a key to his house. I come and go like I live here. I sleep here more than I sleep at my own place. I go to his parent's house for family dinners every week, and now I have the opportunity for a job that's so much more than a job.

I cover the food to keep it warm and sit down on the couch. Cody's late, but that's not unusual. He's a doctor; he has important work to do.

How did I end up with a freaking doctor?

I look around his house. It looks more lived-in than it did when we first met. A piece of art that we found at a gallery hangs above the fireplace, and I got him set of striped curtains. There's a container of stainless-steel cooking utensils next to the stove, and a bowl of produce beside the sink.

His mom gave him some framed pictures for his birthday last month, and he has them sitting out on the mantle. His brother Ryan took them. One is the two of us on the beach. I'm smiling really big, my arms around Cody's neck. He's looking at me, rather than at the camera. Another is Cody with his parents, and the third is the whole Jacobsen clan—plus me. Ed and Maureen, Ryan and Nicole, Hunter, Cody, and me on the end.

I get up and take the photo down off the mantle. What am I doing in this family picture?

The door opens and I jump, almost dropping the photo. I set it on the mantle and swallow back the traitorous tears that threaten to spill down my cheeks.

"Hey, sunshine." He sets his keys down. "It smells amazing in here."

"Thanks." I head for the kitchen and uncover the food. The squash needs a quick stir, but the chicken looks okay.

He stands behind me and rubs my arms, leaning down to kiss my head. The way he touches me is so familiar and safe. Like we've always done this. Like maybe we always will.

But there's no such thing as *always*.

"I wish you would have told me you'd be so late," I say.

He steps back, and I take the chicken to the table.

"Sorry." He sounds surprised. "I was doing some research for a patient."

"Would it kill you to text me? I told you I'd be here and you never even answered."

"I'm sorry; I was busy. I didn't check my phone until right before I left, and then I figured I was going to see you in five minutes anyway, so I just came home."

"It's fine. Let's just have dinner. The chicken probably got too dry, though."

Cody's brow furrows, like he knows what it means when a woman uses the word "fine." But he helps me bring the rest of dinner to the table, and opens a bottle of wine.

My hands tremble as I get two wine glasses out of the cupboard. I feel out of control, like the world is spinning too fast. How much longer can this last? Me, playing house with a doctor. It's kind of ridiculous when I think about it.

I hear the tinkle of glass and gasp. One of the wine glasses is in pieces on the floor at my feet. "Shoot. I knew I was going to drop it."

I look at the shards of glass, and it hits me: the tingle I felt at the café wasn't about the job. It was about my life.

This isn't me. The nice house with pretty family pictures, the career that's more than a job, the responsible man in a tie. I don't belong here, and it's only a matter of time before it all goes away.

"I have to go." I put the other glass down on the counter and dash out the front door.

21

CLOVER

I hear Cody calling for me, but I get in my car and drive away. Tears stream down my face. What was I thinking? Why would a man like Cody Jacobsen stay with me? No one stays with me.

Not even my own parents.

I park in front of my house, not quite sure how I got here. Cody's car is right behind me.

He opens my passenger side door and gets in. "Clover, what's going on? You're not upset about the glass, are you?"

I grip the steering wheel. "No."

"Listen, I'm really sorry about being late. I've been taking you for granted. I know you'll wait, so I don't make myself leave work when I should."

"No, that isn't it. I don't mind that you were late. Not really."

"I made this mistake before. I don't want to do the same thing to you."

"It's not about you being late."

"Okay. Then what's wrong?"

I don't know how to explain it to him. What am I

supposed to say? Your family is too nice to me? You're going to realize I'm not enough for you, and it's going to kill me when you leave?

I glance at my little house. It's a nice place to live, but maybe I was wrong about Jetty Beach. Maybe this isn't where I'm supposed to go. I came here on a whim. I thought I was following fate, but I don't understand where fate is trying to take me.

"I met the head chef of the Ocean Mark today. I made him an omelet."

"That's ... good?"

"He asked me to come see him at the restaurant. He's looking for a sous chef."

"Clover, that's amazing." He reaches out and puts his hand on mine. "Is that what upset you?"

I shrug my shoulders.

"Baby, that's exciting. You're a fabulous cook. This could be a great opportunity."

"I know."

"Are you worried you won't be good enough?" he asks, his voice soft.

Yes. In every way imaginable. "I guess. It just took me by surprise, and I wanted to tell you, but then it felt so scary."

Cody puts a finger beneath my chin and turns my face toward him. "You're a talented cook, and if this seems like something you want to pursue, I think you should. You'd be incredible. It's like you were made for it." His hand slides to my neck, his skin warm against mine.

"Yeah?"

"Absolutely."

"I'll probably drop something."

"How many times have you dropped something at Old Town?"

"I guess just once. That must be some kind of a record for me."

"See? You're not nearly as clumsy as you think you are."

I give him a weak smile.

"Clover, you're special. You light up the world—especially my world. You don't have to be afraid when good things happen to you."

I lean across to kiss him. "You always know the right thing to say."

"Will you come home?"

My breath catches. His home isn't mine, but I know he doesn't mean it that way. "Sure. I'm sorry."

His lips feel exquisite as he kisses me again. "Let's just go eat. We'll both feel better."

I nod. I know what else will make me feel better. Dinner can wait a little while.

I DRIVE NORTH up the highway, heading toward the Ocean Mark. It's one of the nicest restaurants on the entire Washington coast. Cody took me once and the food was amazing. I still can't quite believe I'm going there to talk to the head chef about a job.

I was up-front with Natalie, asking for a day off so I could meet with Gabriel. She was thrilled for me. I told her it might not come to anything—after all, I have no actual training. I only know what a sous chef does because I looked it up. I watched a ton of YouTube videos over the weekend, but I'm still jittery.

The restaurant is built into the side of the hill on the ocean side. It looks like a big lodge, with thick timbers and a tall totem pole outside. There's only one car in the small parking lot. It's early, before their lunch service begins, so they aren't open yet.

Wide double doors lead into the lobby. The lights are dim and there's a big gas fireplace surrounded by river rock. Stairs go up to the lounge on one side and I can see through to the back, where floor-to-ceiling windows display the incredible view of the ocean.

I wait near the host station, not sure if I should go in and look for Gabriel.

It isn't long before he comes out, wearing a white chef's coat. He wipes his hands on a towel and smiles. "Clover, I'm glad you could make it."

"Thanks for having me."

"Let me show you around."

He leads me through the restaurant, showing me the seating areas and the upstairs lounge, then brings me back down to the kitchen. It's like a stainless-steel dream. Long countertops, gorgeous appliances, everything sparkling clean. He shows me around, pointing out where things are kept, and tells me a bit about how it works during a service.

"This is beautiful."

"Thanks. I built it out myself, which was really exciting. I was finally able to create a kitchen that was everything I wanted."

"I've never been in a kitchen like this before."

"So, you already told me you never went to culinary school. Why don't you tell me a little more about your job history."

I try not to cringe as I tell him about the places I've worked. "I know how that makes me look, but I've moved around a lot."

He shrugs. "I don't know, it sounds like you've had a lot of interesting experiences. There was a time in my life when

I was pretty transient. But what about now? How long have you lived out here?"

"Almost six months. And I really love it here."

"Me too. So, that omelet you made me was fantastic—showed a real knack for mixing flavors and textures. How would you feel about cooking something else, here?"

I glance around. "Sure, I guess. What would you like me to make?"

He smiles. "Surprise me."

A flutter of nervousness runs through my tummy as Gabriel walks out of the kitchen, leaving me alone. What am I supposed to do now?

I look through all the food in the giant refrigerators and multiple pantries. There's so much. I think back on the meal I ate here.

The Ocean Mark specializes in seafood. They source local ingredients. He'd want something fresh, vibrant.

I get to work.

I poach a salmon fillet in white wine and butter. The wine will infuse the salmon with a subtle flavor without overpowering the good, fresh taste of the fish; the butter will give the sauce some heft, and a luxurious mouth-feel. Plus, let's be honest: everything tastes better with butter. I add a few sprigs of fresh dill while it simmers, knowing it will be just the perfect little kick to pull the whole dish together.

For a side, I decide on sautéed green beans with garlic—super simple, but big on wow factor if you blister the beans and garlic just right without burning them. My heart beats uncomfortably hard while I cook, but I keep my hands steady and don't break anything. I squeeze half a lemon over the beans; it would be more conventional to add lemon to the salmon sauce, but that dish is already just the right side of busy—and anyway, since when am I conventional? The lemon will be a bright, fresh contrast to the almost-charred elements.

When the food is done, I plate it as nicely as I can, garnishing with a purple kale leaf and a slice of lemon for color. The salmon looks perfect, flaky and moist, and the green beans are exactly right. I can smell the garlic and lemon, their flavors mixing nicely with the dill and white wine.

I find Gabriel at a table right outside the kitchen door. I put the plate in front of him, and have to make myself stay. I'm so nervous I want to run and hide.

He takes a bite of the salmon, and I can see his mind working. He tastes it carefully, his brow furrowed like he's concentrating on the flavor. He doesn't say a word, but takes a bite of the green beans, then puts down his fork.

Oh no. He hates it.

"I'm sorry, have a seat," he says, gesturing to the chair across the table. "I didn't mean to make you keep standing there."

I sink down into the seat and fold my hands in my lap.

"This is delicious."

I let out the breath I didn't realize I was holding. "Really?"

"Yes. This is everything I love in a salmon dish. Cooked perfectly, and the flavors are sublime. You didn't overdo it, which is the biggest problem most inexperienced chefs have. This is subtle."

"Thank you."

"I realize you have a lot to learn, since you've never worked in a real kitchen before. But it's the slow season, so the timing is perfect. I can bring you in a few days a week for the lunch service and start teaching you. By the time summer comes around again, I think you'll be ready. What do you think?"

"You really want to hire me?"

"Absolutely. You're a natural. I'm not stupid enough to pass up on that kind of talent."

"I don't know what to say."

He smiles. "You could say you accept."

I put a hand to my mouth to stop from laughing. I shouldn't be giggling, but I can't help it. "Yes, I definitely accept."

Gabriel reaches out a hand, and I take it. "Great. Lori, my business manager, will give you a call to work out the details. I'm sure you'll have to work out your schedule with Natalie at the café, but you're welcome to start anytime."

"I'll talk to Natalie and let you know. Thank you so much. Really. I'm kind of beside myself right now."

"I have a good feeling about this. I've been looking for the right person for a while now. It kind of seems like this was meant to be."

Maybe he's right. Maybe it was.

22

CODY

I'm probably as excited for Clover's new job as she is. It does mean she's busier, since she has to juggle shifts at the café with time at the Mark. She hopes Gabriel will hire her full-time by next summer, but for now she has to work both places. She handles it like a champ, with her usual sparkle. I'm proud of her, and I love seeing her happy.

I still have that medical conference in Portland, and she arranges to take a few days off so she can come with me. She definitely needs the break. I book us a nice hotel, so she'll be comfortable while I'm attending sessions and meetings all day, and tell her to go nuts with the room service.

It's a three-day conference, and the first two days are informative, if a bit dull. I spend the day at the convention center, attending lectures, taking notes, and networking with other doctors. The first night, I take Clover to a great little French restaurant downtown. She looks stunning in a short black dress and bright red heels. We sip wine, and the food is fantastic. Afterward, we go back to our hotel and try out the jetted tub.

The second night is a Saturday, and Clover wants to go out but keep it casual. I change into jeans and a dark blue t-shirt. Clover wears a black shirt with a lacy back, and a fluttery skirt that shows a lot of leg. We grab burgers and beer at a microbrewery, then walk to a bar nearby. There's great music playing and the bartender's pours are generous.

Our table is off to the side. I sip a glass of Jack Daniels, listening to Clover talk about her childhood. Her life is so foreign to me—growing up moving from place to place, without a lot of rules or boundaries. I can tell she misses her parents, and it blows my mind that she hasn't seen them in years.

"How did your parents meet?"

"A concert. They were both tripping on something and woke up in the back of someone's truck together. I think that was it; they were always together after that."

"That's ... wow."

"I didn't know how different they were until I was around twelve. We stayed in one place for long enough that I made a few friends. I went over to another girl's house and I couldn't get over how different her family was. I'll always remember the huge wedding picture in their dining room. Her mom was in this frilly white dress. She looked young."

"Your parents didn't have wedding pictures in the RV?"

"No, they weren't married," she says, and takes another sip of her drink.

"Really?"

"Nope. They didn't believe in marriage."

I sit back, my hand on my glass. "Believe in it? That's a little odd, don't you think?"

"I suppose. I mean, it seems like most people expect to get married someday."

"Don't you?"

"I don't know," she says with a shrug. "I don't think I really believe in marriage either. It's so permanent, you know?"

"Sure, but don't you think, maybe, if you met the right guy..." I trail off, realizing what I'm about to say. Neither of us are ready to have this conversation, not even close. But it does bother me that she's so flippant about marriage. "Never mind."

She pushes my drink toward me. "Okay, serious doctor man. We're supposed to be having fun tonight."

I smile and swallow the rest of my whiskey. She's right. We've both been working hard lately, and I've been looking forward to unwinding with her all day.

"You know what we need? We need shots."

"Baby, I think you're absolutely right." I resolve to stop at two, because I have a breakfast meeting in the morning with several colleagues.

I don't stop at two.

Clover and I stumble out of the bar an hour or so later, laughing so hard we almost can't breathe. I keep my arm around her shoulders, as much to steady myself as her. Her arm is around my waist, her hand beneath my shirt, warm against my skin. We're downtown, and we should be within walking distance of our hotel—but looking around, I'm not quite sure which direction to go.

We turn left and head up the sidewalk. It's well after dark, but it's a mild night and there are still lots of people out. After a few blocks I still don't see our hotel. My head is swimming from the whiskey and I'm not too sure why I was looking for the hotel in the first place.

"Oh my god, Cody," Clover says, stopping. She points up a side street. "Let's go there."

I look in the direction she's pointing. "Club 90? What is that?"

She laughs. "I think it's a strip club."

I'm drunk, but I'm not sure I'm that drunk. "Why do you want to go to a strip club?"

"Come on," she says, pulling me down the street. "Let's live a little."

People mill around outside—not just guys, but couples and groups of twenty-somethings. At first I think it must just be another bar. As soon as we're inside, there's no question where we are. It's definitely a strip club.

In the center is a t-shaped stage with poles at all three ends. Women dressed in nothing but thongs swing around the poles, flipping their hair as they dance. The place is packed, the seats surrounding the stage all taken. Music blares from huge speakers, and the lights are dim. Tables are set around the rest of the floor, most of them full. Women walk around in black lingerie with tiny bowties at their throats, serving drinks; several bouncers stand with big arms crossed over their thick chests.

I want to tell Clover I'm not sure about this, but she grabs my hand and leads me in. I love women as much as the next guy, but I've never been a fan of strip clubs. The dancers can be aggressive, and to be honest, a lap dance has never done it for me. I can't get over the fact that I'm paying for it, and I know the woman doesn't give two shits about me. There's nothing particularly sexy about that, no matter what she looks like.

The vibe in this place is different from other strip clubs I've been to—more of a party atmosphere. I see as many women as men in the crowd, and most of the people at the tables aren't even paying attention to the girls on the poles. They're hanging out like they're at any other club.

Clover finds us a small table and we get a couple drinks. I know I need to stop—it's getting late and I have to get up early. But I can't very well come into a place like this and not order anything.

Clover sits near me, her knees touching mine, and looks around with a mischievous glint in her eye. "What do you think?"

I take a sip of my whiskey. "I think you're the sexiest woman in here."

"Yeah? Maybe you'd like to see me dance like that?" Clover nods toward the woman at center stage, who hooks her leg around the pole and twirls.

"Wait. You've never worked in a place like this, have you?"

She laughs so hard she almost spills her drink. "Oh my god, no. I'd fall on my face."

I put my hand on her bare knee and slide it up her thigh. "That's okay, you don't need to put on a show for me."

She tips her legs apart and smiles.

I'm just about to get up and lead her out the door, determined to find our hotel, when I realize there's someone standing behind me.

"How about a dance, you two?" The woman has a sparkling red bra barely containing a set of huge boobs, and she has a piercing through her belly button.

Clover and I say "Yes!" and "No, thanks" at exactly the same time.

I swing my head around to Clover. "What?"

She stands and licks her lips. "Come on, baby, don't you want to watch?"

"Private room, then?" the woman asks.

Clover grabs my hand and, before I realize what's happening, I find myself ducking behind a curtain at the side of the club. Bewildered, I let Clover push me into an upholstered seat.

The stripper's dark hair is in a ponytail, and she's wearing thick makeup. "I'm Kitty." She turns a seductive grin on Clover and twines her finger through one of Clover's curls. "I love your hair. So wild."

Clover looks at me and giggles.

"So how about it, big boy," Kitty says, looking at me. "You like to watch?"

She nudges Clover down onto the seat next to me and turns around, then flips her ponytail over her shoulder and arches her back, sticking her mostly bare ass in Clover's lap.

Clover laughs again, putting her hands on Kitty's hips. I'm so fascinated, I can't look away. Kitty runs a thumb beneath her bra, tugging on it. Clover reaches up and unfastens the hooks, then slides her hands down Kitty's back.

Oh shit.

Kitty turns and slips off the bra, revealing huge tits that barely move. She glides her hands up and down her body, rocking her hips to the music.

Turning her attention to me, Kitty moves so she's standing with one leg between Clover's, her other leg between mine, semi-straddling us both. She writhes around in front of us, tossing her hair, moving her hips.

I hardly pay attention to her. Clover's skirt is hiked high up her thighs, and I can see her pulse beating in the thin skin of her throat. I put my hand on her leg and lean in to kiss her neck.

"Ooh, you like her don't you," Kitty says. "Come here, cupcake." She grabs Clover's hands so she's standing, and moves her in front of me.

Clover laughs again while Kitty stands behind her and puts her hands on Clover's hips.

"Move with me, gorgeous," Kitty says. "Show your bad boy what you've got."

Kitty stands close behind Clover, her hips up against Clover's ass. They start to move together, swaying to the beat of the music. Clover's eyes are half-shut, her lips parted. Kitty's hands move up Clover's ribs, lifting her shirt. Clover raises her arms, letting Kitty pull her shirt off, leaving her in nothing but a pink bra and that short black skirt.

I breathe hard, grabbing Clover's waist. Kitty presses her closer and Clover widens her stance to straddle over me.

"That's it, cupcake," Kitty says, leaning over Clover's shoulder. "You're sexy as hell, baby girl."

Clover smiles and grinds into my very hard cock. I groan, holding her hips while she moves over the top of me, rubbing her pussy across my groin, her breasts in my face. I wrap my hand around the back of her neck, pulling her mouth to mine.

My head is fuzzy; Clover's body writhing all over has me going crazy. Her tongue tastes like whiskey, and her vanilla scent fills me. I run my hands up her thighs and grab her ass beneath her skirt.

"Ooh, you two are hot," Kitty says.

I'd forgotten she was even here.

Kitty leans over Clover's shoulder. "Go for it, cupcake." Her voice is low. "Do it. I'll cover for you guys."

Clover's eyes widen and her mouth drops open. She reaches down and starts unfastening my pants.

"Wait, what are you doing?" I say, but I don't try to stop her.

Kitty is still behind Clover, but she backs up a little. She meets my eyes and winks while she continues dancing, then turns, arching her back toward us.

Oh fuck, I don't know if I can do this.

Clover gets my pants open and pulls out my cock, squeezing the shaft. She swipes her other fingers between her legs and rubs her wetness onto me. Her eyes don't leave mine.

"We can't do this here," I whisper.

"Yes, we can."

One hand pushes her panties to the side, while she guides my cock in with the other. My eyes roll back in my head. She feels so fucking good, I can barely stand it. She rides me hard, moving her hips, grinding her hot pussy all over me. I dig my fingers into her ass, moving her faster.

"Do it, baby," she says into my ear. "Come in me right here."

I forget where we are and the fact that a stripper named Kitty is a foot away, faking a lap dance. Her pussy contracts, and I unleash. My cock pulses—harder, harder, pouring into her. I can't see; I can't think. There's only Clover, her huge blue eyes right in front of mine, her tongue licking my lips as she comes.

She finishes and we both pause, breathing hard. Her eyes widen in surprise and she covers her mouth, her body shaking with laughter.

"Holy shit," she says, still laughing. She quickly pulls off of me and adjusts her skirt. I fumble with my pants, trying to get my dick back inside before Kitty turns around.

Kitty stops dancing and picks up Clover's shirt. "Oh my god, you guys. I do this five nights a week, and I'm never turned on, but you two... Let's just say I'm off in thirty, and you are going to make my boyfriend a happy man tonight."

I'm so stunned that I have no idea what to say. I pull a bunch of cash out of my wallet and hand it to her without counting it. She thanks me, Clover puts on her shirt, and we walk out of the curtained booth. Kitty's gone before we get halfway across the floor. I don't bother finding another table. I'm dazed, high as shit on the craziest sex I've ever had.

"I think I need some air."

We get out to the street and walk through the people lingering outside. I grab Clover and push her up against the side of the building, leaning my face close to her ear.

"You're fucking insane; do you know that?" I kiss her neck and nip her ear with my teeth.

"You love it." Her hands glide beneath my shirt, caressing my back.

"You bet I do."

23

CODY

I wake up, sprawled sideways across the bed. I'm naked, although I don't remember getting undressed. Even the memory of getting back to our room is hazy. After Club 90, we somehow managed to find our hotel and stumble upstairs to our room. I'm pretty sure we tried three doors before we found ours. I remember Clover covering her mouth to stifle her laughter every time the room key didn't work.

My head hurts and I need water. I get up and pull on my underwear, then grab a bottle of water from the mini-fridge. Clover is face down, her wild hair spilling out across the sheets.

What a night.

I pinch the bridge of my nose. I had way too much to drink. Did we really have sex in a strip club last night? Holy shit, I think we did.

I take a drink of water, and Clover stirs.

"Hey, gorgeous," she says, blinking at me with sleepy eyes.

"Hey. How do you feel?"

"I think I'm still kinda drunk."

I grab her a water, and she sits up in bed, wearing nothing but the sheet.

"Thanks. What time do we have to leave?"

"Checkout is at eleven. I have a breakfast meeting at nine, but it should only take about an hour."

She puts her water on the nightstand and grabs her phone. "Wait, what time is your thing this morning?"

"Nine."

"Oh, no."

"What?"

"It's ten fifteen."

I grab my phone, but the battery's dead. "Are you kidding me?" I fumble for the charger and plug in my phone. My head is pounding.

"I'm sorry. Well, I guess we can just get breakfast on our way out of town."

"Seriously? Missing this makes me look really unprofessional."

"Okay, so just text them and let them know something came up."

"What am I supposed to tell them? Hey, sorry, I overslept because I got drunk and fucked my girlfriend in a strip club last night."

"We went out and had a little too much fun. Who doesn't do that sometimes?"

"Doctors. Doctors don't do that. Fuck, we didn't use a condom last night, did we?"

"Calm down. I told you, I'm on the pill. It keeps me regular. You don't need to use a condom with me; I won't get knocked up."

"Pregnant isn't the only thing you can get from having sex. Trust me. I've seen what happens."

Clover's mouth drops open and her eyebrows draw together. "Fuck you, Cody."

"What?"

"I've been tested, you asshole. Last year, before I moved to Jetty Beach. I'm so fucking clean you could eat off me. Which, you've done, and I don't recall you complaining then."

"Why were you tested? Did you have a reason?" It's a stupid question, and I know it as soon as the words are out. But I can't help it. I'm a *doctor*. It's literally in my job description to think about stuff like this.

"Well, gosh, Dr. Jacobsen, my last boyfriend had these little sores all over his dick. Do you think that might be a problem?"

I glare at her.

"It was the right thing to do," she says, and I can hear the anger in her voice. "I've had sex before. With other guys. Shocking, I know. I wanted to be sure."

She gets up and storms into the bathroom, slamming the door behind her.

I sit down on the edge of the bed and rub my hands up and down my face. What the hell is happening to me? I feel like I don't know who I am anymore. I drove a motorcycle halfway across the state, broke into my neighbor's backyard, had sex in a strip club. I'm trying to keep up at work, but I'm getting buried and my patient roster keeps growing.

I don't know if I can keep doing this.

Clover eventually comes out, but she's quiet as she packs her things. She's angry with me, but I'm not sure what to say to her. I feel like I've sacrificed a lot for her since we got together, and she keeps pushing. She wants to take me farther and farther out of my comfort zone. Where does it end?

More importantly, where is this going? How much longer before she decides the stars are telling her to move on, and she does?

We spend most of the three-hour drive home in silence. I can't stop thinking about our conversation last night. Maybe I'm rushing, to be thinking about marriage. It's only been six months. But I spent two years with Jennifer, and for most of that time, I knew I'd never marry her. I don't want to do that again. It wouldn't be fair to either of us.

I'm at a point in my life where I want a relationship with at least the potential to be forever. I bought that damn three-bedroom house for a reason: I want to fill it. I want a wife—and, at some point, kids. That's always been what I want, and nothing has ever changed that. Jennifer didn't change it, and Clover hasn't either.

Can I see myself having that life with Clover?

She's not the type of woman I ever saw coming. If I'd met her some other way—through friends, or at a bar, or at someone else's party—I don't know what I would have done. Her smile is infectious, and I would have been entranced. But would I have pursued her? Would I have sought out a relationship with someone so wild and free?

I glance at her from the corner of my eye. I honestly don't know.

"You can just drop me off at home," she says when we turn into town. It's the most she's spoken to me during the entire drive.

"All right."

"You don't get to be mad at me. I get to be mad. You're the one who's being a dick."

"Excuse me? How am I the one being a dick?"

"You're acting like I must be radioactive or something.

Oh no, you had your dick inside me without a coat on. It's the end of the world."

"It's not about that."

"Then what is it about? Why have we been sitting in silence for three damn hours?"

"I overslept and missed a meeting, and you act like it doesn't matter. It's my own fault; I'm not blaming you. I'm the dumbass who kept doing shots. But it's easy for you to be flippant about it. You don't understand the pressure I'm under."

"Right, how can silly little Clover possibly understand? She's just a barista."

"I didn't say that."

"You might as well have."

I pinch the bridge of my nose. "That's not what I mean."

"Then what do you mean?"

Before I can stop myself, I blurt out what's really on my mind. "Can you see yourself getting married? Ever?"

"What? Where did that come from?"

"Last night, you said you don't think you believe in marriage. Is that how you really feel?"

"I don't know. Mostly I'm trying to keep my head above water. Why are we talking about this?"

I grip the steering wheel. This conversation is a disaster already. I shouldn't be saying this. "Because I dated Jennifer for a long time, knowing it wasn't going anywhere. And I don't want to do that again."

She looks at me, open-mouthed. "What am I supposed to say to that? That I'll marry you someday? That I'll be a good little doctor's wife?" She covers her mouth and looks away. When she speaks again, her voice is breaking, like she's fighting back tears. "I'm not her, Cody. I'm not that girl."

"What do you mean?" I have to know. "That it would be a no? You can't even consider the possibility of a future with me?"

"I don't know."

"You know what your problem is? You can't stick with anything because you're scared. You're so afraid everyone is going to leave, you do the leaving first."

"Oh, like you know me so well? You know all about me, don't you?"

"What the fuck do you need? Does your horoscope have to tell you first? Do you need to see a fucking sign in the stars? I can't keep doing this if you're just going to take off one day because you think it's time to move on. That's not me. I'm not built that way. I want a life, Clover. I want a future. And I want it here, not moving around like a fucking gypsy."

Tears run down her cheeks. Damn it, I don't want to make her cry.

"If you can't handle me the way I am, I don't know what we're even doing."

Hearing her say that is a punch in the gut. She *is* going to leave. I've done the math before, I know she's never stayed in one place longer than a year. So that means I have what, another six months before she takes off? At the most?

"I don't know what we're doing either."

I turn onto her street, but I don't want to stop. If she gets out, I don't know if I'll ever see her again.

And I wonder if maybe that's for the best.

I pull up to her house and she flies out of the car. In seconds, she's inside.

I back out of her driveway and leave.

When I get home, I drop my stuff by the front door, head

for the kitchen, and pour myself a drink. I sit on the couch and lean my head back, closing my eyes.

Fuck.

Did I really just end things with her?

I think I did.

24

CLOVER

I spend the next couple of weeks in a haze. I keep expecting Cody to call me, but he doesn't. Granted, I don't call him either. I'm not sure if I'm avoiding him because I want him to be the one to make the first move, or if I don't want to talk to him.

Either way, I know I said the wrong thing.

I knew I would. As soon as the subject of marriage came up when we were sitting in that bar, I knew. I tried to be casual about it, but inside my heart was racing. Why was he asking me about marriage?

I couldn't get the image of that family picture on his mantle out of my mind—the one where I don't belong. My limbs felt jittery and I had to put my drink down so I wouldn't spill. I deflected pretty well, and getting drunk is usually a good way to avoid being too serious. But I saw it in his eyes. I saw the damage I did when I said I didn't believe in marriage.

My parents didn't believe in marriage, and I can't deny their values are a part of me. But I've spent my entire adult life figuring out what I believe, who I am. I've had to. I crossed some arbitrary date on the calendar and they decided they were done with me, left me on my own. I've been looking for my place in the world ever since, and deep down, I'm terrified I'll never find it.

Actually, that isn't true. I'm terrified I will find my place, and I won't be able to keep it.

My shift at the café is almost over and my feet are killing me. After a short post-lunch rush, all is quiet, and I have a chance to catch up on the closing list. I'm grateful I don't have to work at the Mark tonight. I love working there, and Gabriel has taught me so much, but working two jobs is wearing on me.

When I'm there, though, I forget how much my feet hurt and lose myself in cooking. I've learned so many new things, and Gabriel gives me lots of opportunities to experiment with new foods and flavors. He's happy with my progress, and already said he'll have me working full-time by spring. Just a few more months, and I can focus on one job.

Will I still be here in the spring?

The itch to move on is so strong. I pour over my horoscope every morning, wondering if it's going to tell me it's time. Will there be a line about new beginnings? About changing scenery? Maybe something about geography—mountains or deserts, somewhere that isn't the ocean. I convince myself ten times a day that I feel the tingle, that fate is trying to tell me something.

I'm starting to wonder if I'm lying to myself.

I grab my purse from under the counter and check my phone, wondering if today will be the day Cody calls me. I shouldn't be disappointed when I find I have no messages. It's a weekday and he's at the clinic. He rarely called during the day when we were together. He goes to work and shuts out the rest of the world.

He's probably not even thinking about me. In a way, I envy his ability to focus like that. I think about him all day long, wondering what he's doing, whether I should call him. Whether there's anything I can say to make this right.

Hunter comes in and I duck into the kitchen. Natalie's out front, so I wait, peeking through the doorway so he won't see me. I don't want to talk to him, especially here. Just seeing him reminds me of Cody, and my tummy rolls over.

I don't know what Cody told his family about me. I assume they all know we broke up. They talk about everything. Maureen probably knew ten minutes after Cody dropped me off at my place.

I haven't heard from any of them either—but why would I? I'm just the ex-girlfriend who'll fade from their memory. Someday, Cody will find the right woman. He'll marry her, and bring her home to his house. His family will stop saying my name.

I need to get out of here—but I have a few more things to do before I can leave, so I bustle around the kitchen, cleaning up. I grab a tray of clean mugs and glance through the doorway again. Hunter takes his coffee to go and leaves out the front door. I sigh with relief and turn to put the mugs away. My foot slips, I lose my grip on the tray, and the entire thing crashes to the floor.

Natalie comes running, and I stare at the broken ceramic.

"Clover, are you okay?"

I put a hand to my forehead. Of course I dropped the mugs. I screw things up. It's what I do.

"I'm not hurt. I'm so sorry."

"It's all right."

She helps me clean up the mess. My hands shake the whole time. Natalie assures me several more times that she's not upset about the mugs. I try to act like it's not a big deal, but I'm fighting back tears and I don't want to lose it in front of her. As soon as I can make a graceful exit, I leave out the back and head home.

I know what I have to do the moment I walk in the front door.

I was crazy to think I could have this life. Of course I'm going to mess it up. I always do. Cody left me, like I knew he would.

I'm not the kind of woman he needs. I'm a walking disaster. I act on every whim that comes into my head, without thinking things through. I'm terrible at being a grown up. I forget to pay my bills, and I can pack everything I own into a two-door car.

Cody is mature. He's serious. He wants a grown-up life. I never could have given that to him, and I was kidding myself to believe I could.

I'll have to call Gabriel and thank him for the opportunity. But I should get out before I mess things up there, too. I'll break something, or burn the food in the middle of a busy service, or dump soup on the wait staff. It's inevitable. He'll realize I'm not cut out for the job, and that will be it. It will be over.

I pack what I can into some bags and toss them in my car. There's more inside, but I can't deal with it. My landlord can have it, or toss it, or give it away. I'll call her when I get to wherever I'm going. I should be able to pay for next month, so she'll have time to find a new tenant. She'll be fine.

I drive through town, my heart beating hard. I'm breathing too fast, and it's making me dizzy. I have no idea where I'm going. I didn't bother to figure it out. I should have a destination, but I can't think clearly.

I'll just drive until I can't drive anymore. Then I'll sleep and drive again. I don't even care which direction. Maybe I'll head south. There are miles and miles of freeway if I go south. I can put as much distance between me and this town as I need. I can keep going until the world changes, and I'm not the girl no one would ever want to keep.

I'm falling asleep when I finally pull into a cheap hotel off the freeway. I have no idea where I am, only that if I keep driving I'm going to kill myself—and maybe someone else.

The room is musty, but I don't have the energy to care. I fall into bed, still dressed, and go to sleep.

Lies are harder to deny in the morning.

When I'm tired and scared, it's easy to believe the story I tell myself. That fate is guiding me. That I had no choice but to go. That I can't stay even if I want to.

In the morning, in the full light of day, with a surprisingly decent night's sleep behind me, I have to face the truth: I don't want to leave Jetty Beach.

I've followed what I thought were signs, leading me from place to place. But I can find a sign in anything. I can find a reason to move in the wind, in the sky, in a painting in a restaurant. Do I really believe those things have been speaking to me? Or do I just want to believe, so I don't have to take responsibility for my life?

That thought hurts like a punch in the nose.

I get back in my car and sit in the parking lot, watching the cars speed by on the freeway—one set of lanes going north, the other south. I could keep driving south. I've never been to California. Maybe it's time.

I shake my head. Maybe it's time I start making my own choices.

I love my new job, and I don't want to leave it. I might drop something. I might mess up. But I'm also pretty good at what I do and I have a boss who believes in me. Going back is a risk. Something might change, and I might get fired. Gabriel might discover I'm not the right fit and ask me to leave. Or he could hire me full-time and keep teaching me, and it could be the best job I've ever had.

If I don't go back and take the risk, I'll never know.

I think about Cody and my chest hurts. I said the one thing I knew would push him away. But it wasn't because I can't see myself marrying him someday. It was because I *can* see it. I can see it all: the church, the white dress, the framed photo on our dining room wall. It's what I want more than I've ever wanted anything in my entire life. But I'm afraid.

Afraid he'll be another person who leaves me behind.

My own parents didn't want me. Why would he?

I don't want to cry again, but the tears come anyway. I'm sick of crying. I'm sick of waiting for signs. I'm sick of taking stupid risks that don't mean anything, and being afraid to take the risks that really matter.

I drive out of the parking lot and get on the freeway. Northbound. I know what I'm going to do. I don't call him—he's at work already, so he won't answer if I do. But I'll be there when he gets home. Maybe he'll still reject me. I have to steel myself for that. But if I don't try, I'll never know. And if I don't know, I'll live with the regret for the rest of my life.

I don't want to live that way anymore.

25

CODY

I have a break between patients, so I eat a sandwich at my desk and check over Lyle Brown's test results. The last time I saw him, I was able to rule out a number of things. I decided to look past the obvious and I checked him for several autoimmune diseases. Surprisingly, many of his symptoms lined up with polymyalgia rheumatica, a condition that causes pain and limited mobility in the neck, shoulders, and sometimes hips. It wasn't something I expected to see in a man his age. Lyle's only in his forties, and it typically doesn't present in men younger than sixty—and it's more common in women.

But something told me to pursue it, so I ordered an MRI. What I found was inflammation consistent with polymyalgia rheumatica. His blood work pointed to the same. He came in for another appointment, and I decided to trust my instincts. My gut was telling me this was right, even if he didn't fit the profile completely. I started him on a low-dose corticosteriod two weeks ago, and had him come back for blood work. His test results indicate a sharp reduction in inflammation, which is a great sign. I'm anxious to see how he's feeling.

As soon as I come into the exam room, I can tell the treatment is making a difference. Lyle sits up straighter, and he's not flexing his hands. His wife sits next to him, her hand on his arm.

I shake hands with both of them. "Lyle, how are you feeling?"

"So much better, Dr. J. It took a few days, but the pain is almost gone."

His wife beams at me. "Thank you so much. It's so wonderful to have him feeling better."

I take a seat on my stool and run through his test results one more time. "Your blood work looks great. The signs of inflammation are down, and that's exactly what we were looking for. We're going to keep you on the same dose for another two weeks, and then we'll need to gradually reduce it. This will take months, so be prepared for that. We can't reduce your dosage too quickly, or we risk a relapse. But there are side effects—we talked about those at your last appointment. Ideally, a few months from now we'll be able to back you off the steroid completely and only use it again if your symptoms start to return."

"Sounds good, Dr. J."

"So in the meantime, keep working on getting your strength back. And, Mrs. Brown, make sure he's eating well. Inflammation in the body has a lot to do with what we put in it, so his symptoms are less likely to come back if he follows an anti-inflammatory diet. I'll send you more information about that when I get to my office so you'll know what foods to avoid."

Mrs. Brown nods. "Of course. We'll do whatever we have to do."

"Good. I'd like to see you in about sixty days for some follow-up blood work, just to be sure. You can schedule that with Maria or at the front desk."

I stand and Lyle holds out his hand. He shakes with a firm grip. "Thank you again. I can't tell you what it means to me that you didn't give up on me."

"You bet. I'm only sorry I didn't get to the bottom of it sooner. What you're dealing with isn't common, so it took some digging to figure it out."

"It's all right, Dr. J. I'm just glad we found something that works."

"Me too. You guys enjoy the rest of your day."

I avoid walking by the nurse's station on my way back to my office. I'm oddly choked up after seeing Lyle. I'm pleased that the treatment is working, but that isn't what has my throat feeling thick. I figured out his problem because I listened to my gut. I trusted my instincts.

I didn't do that months ago when he first came to see me. I did everything by the book, assuming the book knew what it was talking about. But that doesn't always work, because people aren't their symptoms. They don't fit into neatly detailed lists you can check off to find the answer.

Clover taught me that.

I don't suppose she intended to. But she pushed me to take chances, and to look at the world through different eyes. To draw outside the lines once in a while. I needed that.

Since Portland, I've fallen right back into the habit of living at the clinic. I go in early, and stay late. The staff has noticed, and Darcy called me out on it. I told her I was busy and need to catch up. It's not a lie. But it's not the real reason I haven't left work before eight in weeks. At work, I can focus on my patients. I don't have to think about Clover.

I go back to my office and shut the door, then glance at my phone. I haven't tried to call her. I should. I should swallow my stupid pride and go see her. Maybe she's not ready to think about the future, but does that mean a future isn't possible? I wanted her to assure me she wouldn't bail. But did I give her a reason to stay?

I have two more patients that afternoon, but as soon as I'm finished with the second one, I head out. I drive straight to Clover's house, but it's dark and her car isn't there. Old Town Café is closed in the evenings, but she could be working at the Mark. I drive the twenty minutes up the coast to the restaurant, but I don't see her car. I check with the host to see if she's there, but he tells me she doesn't work today.

Back at her house, I know what I'm going to find. I know she's gone. I park in her driveway and sit there, staring at her front door. No lights. I wonder how long ago she left.

I could call her and ask where she went, but I'm afraid to find out. I want to go inside and find her things still there—her clothes in the closet, her fluffy blue blanket on the couch, her vintage kitchen timer that makes the most horrible noise when it dings. I want to believe they'll be there, that she didn't go.

I know they're not.

I let myself in anyway and look around. The furniture is there, but it was part of the rental. Her things aren't. I open the kitchen drawers and find most of them empty. Her closet is bare. The bed is still made, and the drawer of my t-shirts is still full. But the rest is gone.

So is she.

I leave, locking the door behind me, and get back in my car. I'm as empty as her dark house. I let this happen. I pushed her away and she left. She could be anywhere by now, following the stars.

I glance at my phone. I want to call her, but I don't think I can. I don't want to hear about the signs she followed, or how fate was telling her it was time. I want to tell her I'm sorry—but tonight I don't have the words.

Instead, I drive home, feeling the emptiness eat at me.

At home, I crack open a beer. I haven't moved the pictures my mom gave me. Clover is still on my mantle, smiling at me. That amazing smile. The one that turns on the sun in the morning.

God, I miss her.

I go to work the next day and keep my brain in doctor mode. I see my patients, do my job. I try my best to put Clover out of my mind so I can focus, but she creeps in every time there's a lull. After my last patient, I bury myself in paperwork. Anything to keep my mind off her.

Around six my phone lights up with a text. For a split second, I'm hopeful, but then I see who it's from.

Jennifer.

Hi, sorry, I know it's been a while. I just wanted to check in and see how you're doing.

I blow out a breath. What is she up to? *I'm fine. You?*

Her reply comes quickly. *Ugh. My parents are here and my mom is driving me crazy. Any chance you'll come get a drink with me?*

I wince. Her mother makes Jennifer's life a living hell when she's in town. I debate for a minute before answering. I can tell what she's doing. She wants a reason to get out of the house, and probably needs someone to talk to. Do I want to do this? I suppose it won't hurt anyone to have a drink with her.

Sure.

I meet Jennifer at the Porthole Inn. She looks as put-together as always. Perfect makeup, perfect outfit. I look comparatively under-dressed, in a pair of casual slacks and a green shirt.

She's already at a table when I arrive. I order a drink, but I'm not particularly hungry, so I decline her offer of an appetizer.

It takes me all of three seconds to realize I don't want to be here.

"Thanks for this," she says. "You know what my mom is like. She's been here for two days and I'm going out of my mind."

"I bet."

"So, how have you been?"

"Fine. The clinic is busy, but I guess that's no surprise."

"I take it, since you're out with me, that you aren't seeing that woman anymore?"

I shift in my seat. "That isn't something I want to talk to you about."

She sips her drink. "Fair enough. I was just curious."

"What about you? "I guess wanting to meet me for a drink means you aren't seeing anyone."

"No," she says, her dark red lips curling in a seductive smile. "You're a hard act to follow."

I take a deep breath. A year ago, this would have ended with us having sex, and I'd have found myself right back where I started. I'm not going there, regardless of whether or not Clover is gone for good. "Sorry Jen, but there's no way this is happening."

"What?" she asks, her voice thick with mock innocence. "There's nothing happening."

I raise an eyebrow at her. "I'm sorry your mom is a pain in the ass, I really am. And it doesn't matter if I'm with someone else or completely single. We're not getting back together."

She shrugs one shoulder. "I'm not suggesting we do. But don't you get lonely?"

"How do you know I'm not still with Clover?"

"You're here, aren't you?"

I look away.

"See? Come on, Cody. We might have been at each other's throats too often, but that's because we had passion. Don't you miss that?"

"Not really."

She laughs, as if I'm joking. "Tell you what, let's just go back to your place. Just for tonight. We're both single, there's nothing stopping us. We were good in bed together, at least."

No, we weren't. "Jen, this was a mistake. I'm not bringing you back to my place for some kind of old time's sake hook up." I take out my wallet and toss a twenty on the table. "I'll buy your drink, but I have to go."

"Cody," she says as I walk away. "Cody, you are not walking away from me."

Yes, I think. *Yes I am.*

26

CLOVER

The *Welcome to Jetty Beach* sign is the best thing I've ever seen. I was gone for less than twenty-four hours, and I didn't even tell anyone I was leaving. But driving through the town's gateway feels momentous.

It feels like home.

When I feel the tingle run up my spine, I tell myself I'm just being silly. I want to feel it, so I do. I'm excited, because I can go back to my cottage and unpack my things and pretend I didn't drive seven hours south yesterday.

I can go see Cody.

It's late afternoon, and I don't want to bother him at work. I'll wait until tonight and go to his house. I think about texting him first, to see if he's busy, but I feel like I need to see him in person for this.

I unpack my car, and answer a text from Gabriel. He doesn't need me to come in until Saturday. I smile as I reply. I get to tell him sure, I'll be there Saturday. I don't have to try to explain that I'm gone.

By six, I can't wait anymore. I assume Cody is at work, so I drive to the clinic, but I don't see his car. He's not at home, and I drive by his parent's place but don't find him there either. I kind of feel like a creepy stalker, so I decide to go into town and grab something for dinner. I'm tired from driving so much in the last two days, and I don't particularly want to cook.

I'll just have to break down and call Cody when I get home. I wanted to surprise him, but maybe we'll just have to make plans to get together. That's the mature thing to do anyway, right? A little more planning, a little less spontaneity. I hope I can convince him to see me. We left things so unfinished, I'm not even sure if it was me who was mad, or him. Or both.

My heart leaps into my throat as I drive past the Porthole Inn. I see his car parked outside. There aren't many other cars in the parking lot, but maybe he's having dinner with his family.

I find a parking spot and stop myself before I get out. I'm being impulsive again. Should I interrupt him when he's at a restaurant? What if he isn't happy to see me? That would be humiliating.

But I have to risk it.

I go inside and look around. Several tables are full, but I find him. His back is to me. With a deep breath, I straighten my shirt, my tummy tingling with nervousness. I take a step toward the table and stop dead in my tracks.

He isn't alone.

He's sitting with Jennifer. She takes a sip of a drink, her mouth turning up in a smile. I know that smile. That's an *I want you to fuck me* smile.

I'm going to vomit.

I bolt outside before they can see me. He's with his ex. Did he get back together with her? I can't decide if I want to scream or cry.

My tires squeal on the pavement as I get back on the road. I want out of there. The last thing I need is to see them come outside together.

My thoughts race. *Damn it, Cody, you shouldn't be with her. She's doesn't understand you the way I do. She's cold and selfish and never made you dinner. She'll complain when you work late, even though the work you're doing is incredible. She'll fill up your house with her gallons of makeup and stupid cute shoes and scathing judgment. You'll wake up to that resting bitch face every morning. Is that what you want?*

I want to call him and tell him not to make this terrible mistake. But for all I know, he already made it.

I'm supposed to open at the café in the morning, so I decide to go home. I try to ignore the sick feeling in my stomach, but it won't go away. I don't know if it ever will.

27

CODY

*R*yan texts me Saturday afternoon to see if I want to meet him for a beer. I haven't seen my brothers in a while, so I decide I ought to make myself get out of the house and join them. We meet at a restaurant on Main Street, just up the road from Old Town Café. I haven't been in the café since I left Clover. I avoid looking at it when I drive by.

Hunter's at a window booth when I get there.

"Hey," he says as I sit down.

"Hey man." I notice something on his shirt. "What's that?"

He looks down. "What?"

"You have something on your shirt."

"That's awkward."

"Is that lipstick?"

"Um, yes?" he says, like he's unsure.

I raise my eyebrows at him. I didn't know Hunter was seeing anyone. "What's going on?"

He shakes his head. "It's actually nothing. I, um, kind of hooked up with someone, but it was a stupid thing to do."

"Who is she?"

Hunter looks away and rubs his head with his hand. He looks uncomfortable. "It's nothing."

"All right, man." Hunter's been back in town for less than a year after his medical discharge from the Marines. Until recently, I thought he was adjusting to post-military life pretty well. But beneath his easy smile, there's something else going on. It's clear he doesn't want to talk about it, so I don't push. But I'm also not going to let him close off entirely.

We're guys, there's only so much we want to talk about what's going on in our lives, or inside our heads, and I get that. But I also let my other brother Ryan drift away when he was suffering from depression, and things got bad. Really bad. I'll be damned if I let it happen to Hunter.

As if on cue, Ryan shows up and sits down in the booth. "Hey look, it's brother bonding hour."

The waitress comes by with three beers.

"I ordered for us when I got here," Hunter says.

"Thanks, man," Ryan says.

"So what's up with you?" I ask, looking at Ryan. I want to avoid talking about me, and Hunter seems to be in the same place. I'm hoping Ryan can fill in the conversation.

"Dude," he says with a half-smile on his face. "Nicole and I hung out with Melissa and her fiancé the other day."

"The rich guy?" Hunter asks.

"Yeah, Jackson," Ryan says.

"What was that like?" Hunter asks.

"You know what, the guy's pretty cool. Nicole talked me into it, because Mel's her best friend. I was dreading it, but Jackson's all right." Ryan pauses, his mouth turning up in a grin. "He let me drive his car."

Hunter laughs. "What does he drive?"

"A Bugatti."

I raise my eyebrows. That is a seriously expensive car, with a price tag that starts with an *M*. "Holy shit."

"*Holy shit* is right," Ryan says. "It's the sexiest motherfucking car. Made me want to be a damn billionaire just so I can have one."

"They're getting married too, aren't they?" Hunter asks.

"Yeah, but not until November. Nicole and Melissa planned it all out yesterday over lunch, figuring out the dates so the weddings are far enough apart or whatever. They talked for at least an hour. Jackson and I just sat there looking at each other, all bewildered, while our fiancées planned out our lives. I guess money doesn't make you immune to that."

"Great, more weddings," I say.

"What's your problem?" Ryan asks.

"Cody's pouting," Hunter says.

I lean back in the booth. "For fuck's sake, I'm not pouting."

Ryan looks at me and narrows his eyes. "So are you going to tell us what's going on? Or do we have to keep relying on Mom's guesses?"

"Mom's guesses? Why is she even guessing anything?"

"Because you keep missing dinner with her and Dad," Ryan says. "It's kind of obvious you're avoiding everyone."

I don't want to say it. They already know. I can tell they know. It isn't like news doesn't travel fast in this town. They've been holding back, avoiding asking me questions, and I'm glad of it. If I say it out loud, it will be real. And they're going to ask why. I'm not sure if I have a good answer to that question.

But at this point, it's kind of stupid not to talk about it.

"I broke things off with Clover."

Hunter doesn't say anything, but Ryan raises an eyebrow at me.

"Seriously?" Ryan asks.

"Yes, seriously."

"What did you do that for?" Ryan knows how to push my buttons almost as much as Jennifer did.

"It's none of your goddamn business," I say.

"Of course it's my goddamn business," Ryan says. "You're my brother, and when you're being a fucking idiot it's my job to tell you."

I grind my teeth together and look out the window.

"Don't get pissed at me," Ryan says.

"I'm not pissed at you." And I'm not. I'm pissed at myself. "Look, she was great. But she's..." I trail off. I don't know how to explain it.

"Not the perfect doctor's wife?" Ryan says.

"What the fuck does that mean?"

"Cody, you play it safe. You always have. Clover was a risk. And hey, I don't know what's going on behind closed doors or whatever, but you seemed good together. Really good. And now you're back to living at your clinic and being goddamn pissy all the time. It seems like you were better off with her." He takes a drink of his beer. "But what do I know?"

I stare at the bottle in front of me. "It doesn't matter at this point, because she's gone. She left town. And honestly, that's part of the problem. She's never stayed anywhere in her life. She doesn't stick things out. She sees some fucking sign in the clouds and she takes off. That's not me. I don't want to pack up and move to a new place every time I get bored. I need someone who's dependable."

"She didn't leave town," Ryan says.

"Yes, she did."

"No, she didn't," Ryan insists. "I saw her at the café. She was working."

I sit up in my seat. "When?"

"Yesterday. She asked if you were doing okay, but she looked pretty upset when she said it."

"That's so weird. I went to her place to talk to her, and she was gone."

Ryan shrugs. "I don't know. Maybe she just wasn't home when you stopped by. But I definitely saw her."

She's still here. That means she didn't bail. She didn't move on.

Hunter looks out the window and his eyes widen. "Holy shit."

Tires screech and there's a loud crash, the sickening crunch of metal on metal.

Before I process what's happening, I'm out the door, Hunter and Ryan on my heels. Two cars are in the middle of the intersection—one silver, the other red. The front of the silver car is smashed into the driver's side of the red one. Behind me, I hear Hunter say something about the silver car coming out of nowhere and running the stop sign.

Clover drives a red car.

I run, sprinting toward the scene. There's no way it's her. She left. I don't give a shit what Ryan said, she left town. She's long gone, so she can't be in that car. It can't be her.

I get closer. Smoke or steam rises from the silver car and a guy stumbles out. He has blood on his face. I hear Ryan talking to a 911 operator. The guy needs help, but he's on his feet, and I have to get to the other car. The silver car is in the way. I can't see who's driving the red one.

The driver's side is smashed in and blocked. I can't get to it. I run around to the passenger side and rip open the door.

No. No, no, no, no.

Curly blond hair. A long-sleeved yellow shirt. Her eyes are closed.

The side of her car is smashed in, pushing her across the center console, despite her seat belt. Her head lolls to the side, her chin against her shoulder. I smell the tang of blood, and I crawl inside, desperate.

Please don't be dead. Please don't be dead.

"Clover." I feel her neck. There's a pulse, but it's weak. I almost cry with relief. "Clover, stay with me. Stay with me, baby."

Then I see the blood. It's blooming across her yellow shirt and down her pants, darkening her clothes with alarming speed. My chest tightens with panic.

I have to get her out of here.

Time seems to slow, all the details of the car sharpening. My heart is pounding, but I force myself into calmness, pushing away my fear. In my mind, I can already see each action I need to take. Moving her is a risk because of the possibility of a spinal injury, but she'll bleed out if I don't stop it. I have to trust my gut.

My hands are steady as I unfasten her seatbelt and wedge my arms beneath her. I pull her to the passenger's side, holding her body next to mine. Blood seeps onto my sleeves, hot and sticky.

I get her out and lay her down on the road next to the car. Her left arm bends the wrong way; it's broken, but a broken arm won't kill her. I carefully move it out of the way and lift up her shirt to see where the blood is coming from.

There's a ragged gash in her side, just above her hip. Dark blood seeps out. I quickly pull off my shirt and fold it. It's not sterile, but I don't have anything else. I have a first aid kit in my car, but there's no time. I apply it to the wound, careful not to press too hard. I don't want to do more damage and she's probably bleeding internally. There's nothing I can do to stop that, except keep her alive until the paramedics get here.

I hold my shirt against her, firm but gentle. I look up at Hunter. "Push her legs up so her knees are bent, her feet flat on the ground."

He nods and kneels next to her. His face is stoic as he moves her legs up, bending her knees. It puts her in a better position, and she's unconscious so we don't have to worry about the pain.

Blood soaks through the shirt onto my hands. I can still hear Ryan talking to someone, but his voice seems far away. I hold onto her, watching the color drain from her face. I'm a fucking doctor, but I'm sitting in the road and there's nothing else I can do.

The whine of an ambulance siren cuts across the air. In seconds, the paramedics are here, asking me questions. I tell them I'm a doctor, give them my evaluation. My voice is calm and devoid of emotion, but inside I'm holding on by nothing but the thinnest of threads. They ease her onto the gurney, moving as fast as they can. I stand there, covered in her blood, while they load her into the back of the ambulance.

A second ambulance is nearby, helping the other driver. Police cars block the intersection. Lights flash all around me and a smattering of onlookers peer at the scene of the accident from the fringes.

"She's lucky you were nearby," someone says.

I turn to look at the paramedic. The ambulance siren turns on and it starts to drive away.

"She's my girlfriend." It doesn't sound like my voice.

"Cody!" Someone's calling my name. Ryan.

I blink hard, the world around me going blurry. I look down at my bloody hands.

"Cody, let's go."

A cop yells for us to stay. He wants to take a statement. But the paramedic stops him, telling him we're going to the hospital with the victim.

Hunter and I get in Ryan's car. I don't remember how I got here, but I'm sitting in the passenger seat and we're halfway to the hospital before my brain starts to catch up with me. All I can see is Clover's face, going pale, her blood all over my hands. Ryan grips the steering wheel, driving fast, the lines around his jaw tense.

We park outside the entrance to the emergency room. Hunter hands me a t-shirt and I realize I'm not wearing one. It was on Clover. Soaking up her blood. I put it on and get out. I'm in a daze.

Reality hits me upside the head when we walk into the ER, and suddenly I'm coherent again.

"I'm Dr. Jacobsen," I say to the attendant. "I was just at the scene of an accident at the intersection of Main and First in Jetty Beach. Victim was a woman in her late twenties. Severe abdominal laceration, possible internal bleeding, further injuries undetermined. She should have arrived via ambulance in the last five minutes."

The woman nods. "I'll check the status for you." She leaves for a moment, and my heart beats so hard I can barely breathe. She returns. "They already took her to the OR. She's being prepped for emergency surgery right now."

That means she's still alive.

"Would you like to go back and clean up, Dr. Jacobsen?" the woman asks.

I look down at my hands, covered in rust-colored streaks. There's nothing I can do for Clover except wait. I'm not a surgeon. I can't scrub in and assist. Even if I was, I'm in no state for it. It's all I can do to keep from shaking.

"Yeah, sure. Thank you."

A nurse in blue scrubs comes out and leads us back. I hear Ryan tell the nurse the victim is my girlfriend.

Except she isn't. Because I fucking left her.

I clean up in a bathroom, and someone leads us to another waiting room. She says the surgeon will come out when he's finished. She asks us if we want coffee.

I sit down in a chair and lean forward, putting my face in my hands. I smell like the harsh chemical emergency room soap. I still have blood on my pants. My gut churns with fear, and worry, and impotence. There's nothing I can do and I can't get over the feeling that this is my fault. If I hadn't left her, she wouldn't have been in her car today. We would have been at my place. This shouldn't have happened.

Please, Clover. Please don't die.

THE WAIT FEELS LIKE HOURS. Ryan and Hunter stay, and it isn't long before my mom and dad are there. Nicole shows up soon after.

I pace around the surgical waiting room. Mom tries to get me to eat something. Everyone else keeps their distance, giving me space. I've never been so scared in my entire life.

Why didn't I call her? Or send her a text? I should have, even just to see how she was doing.

I never should have left her in the first place.

I know, with every piece of my soul, that she and I were meant to be together. I knew it this morning, before I was pacing in a fucking hospital, waiting to see if she's going to live or die. I knew it when I went to her empty house. I knew it when I dropped her off and let her get away.

The surgeon comes out and looks around at us, as if he isn't certain who he's supposed to talk to.

"I'm Dr. Foster. Are you all here for Clover Fields?"

We all step forward, converging on him. I try to read his face, my gut twisting in a knot.

"Yes," my mom says behind me. "We're her family."

My chest clenches. *Her family.*

"Surgery went well," the surgeon says. "She has bruised ribs, but she's fortunate that none of them cracked. Her left arm is broken in two places, but we were able to set and splint it. That should take four to six weeks to heal. The real problem was the abdominal laceration. Something pierced her abdomen on the left side. I'm confident I stopped all the bleeding, but we'll need to keep her here for a few days at least. She lost a lot of blood, but a transfusion took care of that. All in all, she was very lucky."

I close my eyes. She's okay. I put a hand to my chest. My lungs feel heavy, like I can't get enough air.

"Thank you," I manage to croak out.

"Whoever was first on the scene probably saved her life. She was bleeding heavily, but whoever got to her first did everything right. She's still asleep now, but a nurse will bring you back to see her soon. Although ... maybe not all of you at once."

My legs feel like they might buckle. I shake hands with Dr. Foster and thank him again. I think my family can tell I'm about to collapse, because I feel a strong arm around my shoulders. Hunter. I breathe out a long, slow breath. She's okay. She's going to be fine. I'll be with her soon.

And I'm never letting go of her again.

28

CLOVER

I'm floating, like my head isn't attached to my body. The lights are dim, but still too bright. Everything looks stark. Cold. Sterile. Tubes cross my face, hanging near my eyes. I'm lying on my back, my head slightly lifted. I have no idea where I am.

I suck in a breath, fear gripping me. My eyes won't focus.

"Clover."

Someone says my name. The voice is so familiar, but it feels like a dream. I squeeze my eyes shut and open them again, trying to make sense of what I'm seeing. My head is so fuzzy.

"Clover," someone says again. A hand over mine, squeezing gently. "Baby, can you hear me?"

"Cody?" My voice doesn't sound like mine.

"Yeah, baby, it's me."

It can't be Cody.

"Shh," he says. "Don't talk. You're okay. I'm here. I won't leave."

I close my eyes. I can't stay awake. I don't know where I

am, but Cody's hand is on mine and I relax, drifting back into blackness.

When I open my eyes again, I'm still fuzzy, but at least I can think.

There's an IV in my arm and tubes beneath my nose. I try to move but my breath catches. I feel like I got hit by a truck. Everything hurts. It's a dull pain, the sort that should be sharp and intense, but it's being suppressed by pain killers. That must be why my brain is so cloudy.

The room is dim, but slivers of light shine through the blinds. Machines beep and I can see the drip of the IV fluids next to me. Drip. Drip. It trails down the tube into my arm.

I blink again and realize I'm not alone. Cody's sitting in a chair next to me. He's slumped down, his head resting awkwardly on his shoulder, his eyes closed.

I try to talk, but my mouth and throat are so dry, it's hard to make a sound.

"Cody." My voice comes out as nothing but a croak.

His eyes open and he sits up, grabbing my hand. "Clover. Hi, sunshine."

Images flash through my mind. Memories I can't quite make out. Driving through an intersection. A moment of panic. A flash of silver. Then nothing. Nothing but blackness until I see Cody's face. Every time I open my eyes, I see his face, feel his hand on mine. Through the panic and the fear and the pain, he is there.

"Do you know where you are?" he aska.

"Hospital?"

"Yeah. Do you remember what happened?"

"I'm not sure."

"You were in an accident. A guy t-boned you when you went through an intersection."

"When?"

His brow furrows and he pulls out his phone. "I guess that was two days ago."

"Two days?" It's coming together, but my mind is struggling to catch up. "Am I hurt?"

He squeezes my hand again. "Your arm is broken, and you have a lot of bruises. Something cut you open on your left side. You were in surgery for a couple hours, but they got you all put back together."

Oh my god. Surgery? "Did I hit my head again?"

He smiles. "No, baby, you didn't hit your head. You actually got lucky there. That could have killed you."

"Am I allowed to have water?"

"Yeah, of course. Hang on." He's gone for a moment and returns with a little cup and straw. "Here. Just a sip until we're sure you can handle it."

I take a drink and the cool water feels like heaven in my mouth. It soothes my scratchy throat. I shift my legs and wince as a sharp jolt of pain shoots through me.

"Don't move too much," he says, putting a gentle hand on my shoulder.

I stare at him. How is it possible that he's here? I just woke up. I couldn't have told someone to call him. "How did you know?"

A shadow of pain crosses Cody's face. "I was first on the scene."

"What? What does that mean? How?"

"I was a block away, having a beer with my brothers. Hunter saw it happen out the window. I heard the crash, and I saw the car was red. I ran to the scene. I had to make sure it wasn't you. But it was." He stops and looks away. "I pulled you out of your car and tried to stop the bleeding until the paramedics arrived."

Tears flood my eyes. "Are you serious?"

"Yeah."

"Have you been here this whole time?"

"Yeah, they tried to make me leave overnight, but I pulled rank. One of the good things about being a doctor, I guess."

"Cody, I don't know what to say. I thought..."

He leans forward and touches my arm. "What?"

"I thought you got back together with Jennifer."

His eyebrows draw down and he sits back. "What? No. Why would you think that?"

"I saw you having dinner with her. I saw the way she was looking at you."

"Wait, the other night at the Porthole Inn? You were there?"

"I saw your car, so I went in. But you were with her." My voice breaks on the last word.

He moves close and puts a hand on my face. "Baby, no. She asked me to meet her and I shouldn't have. I left. I didn't even finish my drink."

"But—"

"Wait," he says, putting a finger to my lips. "You're hurt, sunshine. We don't have to do this now."

Sobs bubble up, and my throat feels like it's closing. I can't stop. "You left me."

"Oh fuck, I know," he says. "That was the stupidest thing I've ever done in my life. I'm so sorry."

"No, it was me," I say through sobs. "I made you do it."

"You didn't make me do it," he says, caressing my cheek.

"I did. I ruined it because I was so scared, and I tried to find you to tell you that I was sorry, but you were with her."

"I tried to find you, too. I went to your house, but your stuff was gone. Jennifer texted me the next day and asked me to meet her. I figured ... I don't know, I shouldn't have done it, but it wasn't about you, and it certainly wasn't about being with her."

"You went to my house when I was gone?" *Oh no.*

"I'm sorry. I should have just called you, but I wanted to see you in person. When I got to your house, I thought you left town again. I figured you decided to move on, and I kind of didn't want to know where you went. I should have just called. I'm so sorry."

I sob again. "Oh god, Cody, I did leave. It was so stupid. I drove seven hours and turned around and came home the next day."

He laughs. "You're kidding me."

"No, I really did."

"But you came back."

"Yeah. I didn't want to go."

He moves one of the tubes that's sticking out of me and clasps my hand. "Just relax now. We're both here. You're going to be fine."

The rest of the room comes into focus. There are balloons and flowers everywhere. "Wait, what is all that stuff?"

Cody looks behind him. "I think about half of it is from my mom. She got the yellow balloons and the flowers over there." He picks up a pink teddy bear. "I don't know why she thought you needed this. I guess she kind of went nuts in the gift shop downstairs. Nicole sent the basket of snacks, and there's some lotion and a toothbrush and a few other things in there, too. Natalie sent over a box of muffins and some cookies yesterday—but I have to be honest, I ate some and shared the rest with the nurses. There's more flowers over there on the little table, and I don't even know who sent them all. There are cards with them. One is from Gabriel, I think. He's called a couple of times."

I stare all of it, open-mouthed. I can't fathom what I'm seeing. "This is all for me?"

"Of course it is."

More tears run down my cheeks. I can't possibly stop them.

"No, don't cry."

"I just don't understand any of this. Why would all these people care if I got hurt?"

There's a knock at the door and a man in a white doctor's coat over a shirt and tie steps in. He has gray hair at his temples, and small black glasses perched on his nose. "Mind if I come check on her?"

"Of course not" Cody doesn't let go of my hand.

"Hi, Clover. I'm Dr. Foster. I performed your surgery the other day. I just need to check your sutures."

"Okay."

He comes around to my left side and moves the sheets down. Cody stands and looks over me while Dr. Foster pulls back bandages. I'm too scared to look.

"This is healing very well." He meets Cody's eyes. "What do you think?"

"It looks good," Cody says. "You did excellent work."

A nurse comes in behind Dr. Foster to take off the dressing and put on a fresh one.

"How's your pain level, Clover?" Dr. Foster asks.

"I'm okay as long as I don't move much. I don't know; I feel pretty out of it."

"She hasn't been awake long," Cody says.

"I'm going to keep her here another night," Dr. Foster says. "We'll get her on her feet later today and have her walk around a little. If she's able to get around without too much pain, she can go home tomorrow. But only if she's going to have help. Do you live alone, Clover?"

I start to answer, but Cody cuts me off. "No, she'll come home with me."

"Good. I'm comfortable sending her home with you, probably by about midday tomorrow, as long as she keeps improving." He turns back to me. "Your arm will take four to six weeks to heal, but Dr. Jacobsen here can handle the follow-up for that. Your abdominal wound will be about the same, and it could take several months to feel one hundred percent. It's really important that you take it easy, especially while the laceration is still healing. You were pretty torn up inside, too, so remember: as much damage as you can see on the outside, there was damage on the inside. Listen to your doctor, and you'll be fine. Do you have any questions for me?"

I doubt I could think of them even if I did. My head is swimming, but I know Cody heard it all. "No, I don't think so."

He glances around at the flowers and balloons. "You have a lovely family, Clover. They've really been pulling for you."

Cody thanks Dr. Foster and shakes his hand. My lower lip trembles as I watch him go.

A family?

"Hey," Cody says, sinking back down into his chair. He wipes a few tears from my cheeks. "It's okay. I know six weeks sounds like a long time, but you're going to be fine."

"I believe in marriage."

"What?"

"I told you I didn't, but I lied to you." I feel like I'm slipping again. My eyes want to close, but I have to tell him before I fall asleep. I have to say it. "I said I didn't because I was afraid. You were right. I'm always afraid everyone is going to leave me. So I leave first. But I don't want to leave this time."

"Baby," he says, caressing my face. His hands are so gentle. "If you think I'll let you go again, you're crazier than I thought."

I smile and Cody clutches his chest.

"Yes, that. That right there. My sunshine smile." He brushes his fingers across my lips. "From the first moment I saw you, all I have ever wanted to do is make you smile like that for me."

That makes me smile even more.

"I love you, Clover," he says, his eyes locked on mine. "I love you so much and so big I'm not sure what to do with it. But I know I'm never letting you go again."

I can't keep my eyes open, so I let them drift closed.

"I love you, too, Cody. I love you, too."

EPILOGUE: CLOVER

My face literally hurts from smiling.

The photographer snaps more pictures, then moves us around again. He asks us to hold up our bouquets. Mine is pale pink and white with sweet little pearls. There are matching pearls in my hair, which the stylist somehow managed to tame into soft curls that frame my face and hang around my collarbone. The photographer finally pauses, and I move my jaw around to loosen up my face. I grab the top of my dress and hike it up a bit. It's a gorgeous champagne-colored strapless dress that goes to my knees. It's so pretty, although I worry a little that it's going to slip too far down and show a lot of boob. I guess Cody won't mind.

Nicole turns to me and smiles, taking a deep breath. She's positively radiant. Glowing, even. Her wedding gown is sheer at the top, with tiny floral appliques around the sweetheart neckline. It flows down to an A-line skirt of soft tulle. Her blond hair is done in a simple up-do with a clip holding her veil. Looking at her makes me smile more, even though I kind of need a break after so many photos.

"Are you hanging in there?" I ask.

She bites her lower lip. "I think so. I can't decide if I'm scared or excited."

"Excited, obviously. And you look amazing."

We've been taking pictures with just the women, saving the rest for after the ceremony. Nicole didn't want Ryan to see her beforehand. She looks so beautiful she's going to knock his socks off.

"Yes, excited," she says, taking another breath. "Thanks for being here with me."

"I wouldn't have missed this for anything."

I was stunned when Nicole asked me to be a bridesmaid. Her wedding was only a few months away, and she already had her best friend Melissa as her maid of honor. But she insisted. I certainly couldn't refuse. Truth be told, I squealed and jumped up and down when she asked me. I've never been a bridesmaid before.

I've never even been to a real wedding before.

The photographer tells us it's almost time and leads us to the back of the church. The doors are closed, but soft music drifts through. Melissa and I both hug Nicole for the millionth time and take our places in front of her. Nicole's mom and dad stand on either side of her, and Melissa steps in to straighten her veil and make sure her bouquet is perfect.

I'm so excited I can barely stand it. I do my best not to bounce in my heels.

The doors open and I go first. The men are already at the front, Ryan standing in the center, with Cody and Hunter next to him. Cody looks utterly delicious in his dark gray suit. I wink at him as I walk up the aisle. He grins at me and winks back.

I cry through the entire ceremony.

Epilogue: Clover

Ryan fights back tears as Nicole walks up the aisle. It's so moving, half the audience loses it before the minister even says a word. I can see Ryan's face through the entire thing, and he looks at her with so much passion, it takes my breath away. They say their vows and everyone in the audience who wasn't crying before starts. Anyone who doesn't cry must not have a soul, because it's the most beautiful thing I've ever witnessed. Even Cody looks choked up.

His eyes are on me through the whole thing.

I look at him, standing just past Ryan's shoulder, and smile.

Afterward there are more pictures—lots of them—but soon we're all in a limo, glasses of champagne in our hands, heading to the reception.

Nicole originally wanted the wedding and reception to be in Ryan's photography studio, but their guest list got too long. So they opted for a beautiful church in town for the ceremony, and booked a hotel banquet room for the reception. It's a lovely June evening, so they open the doors to the terrace, and the sound of the ocean carries through. The moon is bright and the waves crash against the sand.

Cody is busy greeting distant family members, so I go outside to get some air. I press at my side, where a shard of metal cut me open. It's only the slightest bit tender now. It aches when I work too much, so I'm careful, but overall I've healed well. I have a scar, but Cody loves to trace it with his fingers or his tongue, so it isn't so bad. It's a good reminder of everything I almost lost.

I've gone back to work at the Mark, but only part-time. It's a demanding job, so I need to pace myself while I'm still recovering from the accident. Gabriel has been nothing but supportive. He's the best boss I've ever had. I did quit my job at the café, but it's still my favorite place to get coffee. I meet

Nicole there at least once a week. She'll be gone for two weeks in the Caribbean on her honeymoon, and I'm really going to miss her.

I take a sip of wine and lean against the railing, watching the waves. My heart is so light after watching Nicole and Ryan get married. I love seeing people so blissfully happy. It gives me hope for humanity.

"Hey, sunshine." Cody comes to stand next to me and puts an arm around my shoulders.

"Hey, handsome," I say, and put my wine glass down on a little table.

He pulls me to him, turning me so our bodies are pressed close together. I thread my arms around his neck and he leans in to kiss me.

He tastes like champagne and his mouth feels decadent. He pulls away, but I don't want him to stop kissing me. Maybe ever.

"So when can we go upstairs to our room?" I ask. "You look so hot in this suit, but I'd really like to take it off you."

He leans in close, his mouth near my ear. "Soon, baby, soon. But we just got here. There's still dinner, and cake, and dancing."

"I might be convinced to stay for cake."

He kisses the top of my head and lets his arms drop, turning back toward the water. I pick up my glass and have another sip, then lean my head on his arm.

He takes my hand and rubs my index finger.

My heart rate picks up.

He moves to my middle finger, rubbing it in slow circles, just above my first knuckle.

I glance at him out of the corner of my eye. His dimples are puckered, but he's looking out at the waves.

He takes my ring finger between his finger and thumb,

rubbing it just like the others. I feel like I can't quite breathe. Is he going to—

He brings my hand to his lips and kisses it. "We should go in. I think they're serving dinner."

I blow out a breath and swallow hard. What was that about?

I take a seat at our table. We're near the front, seated with Hunter and his date, and Melissa and her fiancé. Jackson is one of the most gorgeous men I've ever laid eyes on, and the way he looks at Melissa like he wants to eat her for dinner is kind of a turn on.

We enjoy a delicious meal, and then there are toasts by Melissa and Cody. Melissa's is hilarious and heartfelt, and I almost cry again. Cody's is tender and sweet, but he ends on a funny note that has the whole crowd laughing and clapping. We drink champagne, eat wedding cake, and chat with the people around us.

After the guests eat their cake, Ryan stands up and takes the microphone, Nicole at his side.

"Nicole and I would like to thank everyone for coming," Ryan says. "It means so much that you'd be here to share our special day with us."

There's a soft round of applause.

"Those of you who know our family know that we're pretty close," he says.

I glance over at Maureen and see her beaming at her son. Even Ed, who's usually pretty stoic, has a huge smile on his face.

"We are so happy to be able to welcome Nicole into our family, as the newest Jacobsen."

More applause and a few whistles from the crowd.

"But families are meant to grow." He pauses, his dimples showing as he grins, and there are some gasps.

Holy shit. Is he going to say what I think he's going to say? I reach over to grab Cody's hand, my heart suddenly racing with anticipation. Is Nicole—

But Cody stands up.

"My brother Cody has a little something he'd like to say," Ryan says. He looks at me and meets my eyes with a smile. Nicole has tears in her eyes again, and she puts her fingers over her mouth. She's staring at me. Why is she smiling at me like that?

Slowly, I look up at Cody.

The crowd goes silent. I'm positive they can hear my heart beating.

He reaches for my hand and draws me up to standing. Out of nowhere, he has a microphone.

"Clover, I don't know if it was God, or fate, or the universe who brought us together. But I know one thing with so much certainty, no one could ever convince me otherwise: we were made for each other. We were meant to be."

I cover my mouth with a shaking hand.

Cody sinks down onto one knee and the crowd gasps. I stare at him, blinking through tears. He cannot be serious. At Nicole's wedding?

He takes my hand.

"Clover Fields, in the presence of my family, who insisted I do this here because they love you as much as I do, will you marry me?"

I lower my hand and my face erupts in a smile. I laugh, and I can barely get the words out. "Yes! Yes, yes, oh my god, yes."

He pulls a box out of his pocket and opens it, revealing a pale blue stone set in a platinum band, surrounded by tiny

Epilogue: Clover

sparkling diamonds. It's the most beautiful thing I've ever seen. He stands and slips it on my finger.

I'm vaguely aware of applause and cheering around us, but nothing else exists. Just Cody's arms around me, his lips against mine. Lips that have always been meant to kiss me. Forever.

Fate finally got it right.

AFTERWORD

Dear reader,

If you've read the Jetty Beach romances up to this point, you've probably started to catch on to a theme in the stories I write. Broken people.

There's something so compelling about people who bear wounds and scars, and the ways that love can help them heal. Honestly, who among us isn't at least a little bit broken? One of the main reasons I'm drawn to writing romance is because I believe in the healing power of love. I've lived that in my own life, and it comes naturally to me on the page. People are flawed, and exploring how those flaws influence the choices we make is fascinating to me.

My editor called Clover "beautifully broken," and that's exactly what I meant for her to be. I hope I've done her justice in this book, because she became so special to me. Beneath her optimism and her charming smile, she's a deeply wounded woman who was abandoned by the two people who should have loved her enough to stay in her life. She's left with a very skewed concept of her place in the world—she's always searching, but never finding what she's looking for. And behind that search is a lot of fear.

She comes to realize that her dependence on "fate" is a coping mechanism, and often an excuse. She's terrified of letting anyone get too close to her, lest they leave her the way her parents did. That fear dominates her life until she finally learns to trust in what she has with Cody.

Cody was a departure for me in some ways. There's no sad backstory for Cody. He has a nice family. He's a successful doctor and business owner. Is his life perfect? Of course not, and he's not perfect either. But the brokenness that usually draws me to a character wasn't there for him.

But I realized he was exactly what he needed to be for this story—for Clover. They were both searching for the one to make them whole, the other person to complement their strengths and shore up their weaknesses. And they do this for each other so perfectly. Cody never saw her coming, and Clover couldn't have guessed she'd wind up with a man like him. But sometimes life's little surprises are the most magical things.

I love the magic.

Thanks for reading!

CK

ALSO BY CLAIRE KINGSLEY

For a full and up-to-date listing of Claire Kingsley books visit www.clairekingsleybooks.com/books/

For comprehensive reading order, visit www.clairekingsleybooks.com/reading-order/

The Haven Brothers

Small-town romantic suspense with CK's signature endearing characters and heartwarming happily ever afters. Can be read as stand-alones.

Obsession Falls (Josiah and Audrey)

The rest of the Haven brothers will be getting their own happily ever afters!

How the Grump Saved Christmas (Elias and Isabelle)

A stand-alone, small-town Christmas romance.

The Bailey Brothers

Steamy, small-town family series with a dash of suspense. Five unruly brothers. Epic pranks. A quirky, feuding town. Big HEAs. Best read in order.

Protecting You (Asher and Grace part 1)

Fighting for Us (Asher and Grace part 2)

Unraveling Him (Evan and Fiona)

Rushing In (Gavin and Skylar)

Chasing Her Fire (Logan and Cara)

Rewriting the Stars (Levi and Annika)

The Miles Family

Sexy, sweet, funny, and heartfelt family series with a dash of suspense. Messy family. Epic bromance. Super romantic. Best read in order.

Broken Miles (Roland and Zoe)

Forbidden Miles (Brynn and Chase)

Reckless Miles (Cooper and Amelia)

Hidden Miles (Leo and Hannah)

Gaining Miles: A Miles Family Novella (Ben and Shannon)

Dirty Martini Running Club

Sexy, fun, feel-good romantic comedies with huge... hearts. Can be read as stand-alones.

Everly Dalton's Dating Disasters (Prequel with Everly, Hazel, and Nora)

Faking Ms. Right (Everly and Shepherd)

Falling for My Enemy (Hazel and Corban)

Marrying Mr. Wrong (Sophie and Cox)

Flirting with Forever (Nora and Dex)

Bluewater Billionaires

Hot romantic comedies. Lady billionaire BFFs and the badass heroes who love them. Can be read as stand-alones.

The Mogul and the Muscle (Cameron and Jude)

The Price of Scandal, Wild Open Hearts, and Crazy for Loving You

More Bluewater Billionaire shared-world romantic comedies by Lucy Score, Kathryn Nolan, and Pippa Grant

Bootleg Springs

by Claire Kingsley and Lucy Score

Hot and hilarious small-town romcom series with a dash of mystery and suspense. Best read in order.

Whiskey Chaser (Scarlett and Devlin)

Sidecar Crush (Jameson and Leah Mae)

Moonshine Kiss (Bowie and Cassidy)

Bourbon Bliss (June and George)

Gin Fling (Jonah and Shelby)

Highball Rush (Gibson and I can't tell you)

Book Boyfriends

Hot romcoms that will make you laugh and make you swoon. Can be read as stand-alones.

Book Boyfriend (Alex and Mia)

Cocky Roommate (Weston and Kendra)

Hot Single Dad (Caleb and Linnea)

Finding Ivy (William and Ivy)

A unique contemporary romance with a hint of mystery. Stand-alone.

~

His Heart (Sebastian and Brooke)

A poignant and emotionally intense story about grief, loss, and the transcendent power of love. Stand-alone.

The Always Series

Smoking hot, dirty talking bad boys with some angsty intensity. Can be read as stand-alones.

Always Have (Braxton and Kylie)

Always Will (Selene and Ronan)

Always Ever After (Braxton and Kylie)

~

The Jetty Beach Series

Sexy small-town romance series with swoony heroes, romantic HEAs, and lots of big feels. Can be read as stand-alones.

Behind His Eyes (Ryan and Nicole)

One Crazy Week (Melissa and Jackson)

Messy Perfect Love (Cody and Clover)

Operation Get Her Back (Hunter and Emma)
Weekend Fling (Finn and Juliet)
Good Girl Next Door (Lucas and Becca)
The Path to You (Gabriel and Sadie)

ABOUT THE AUTHOR

Claire Kingsley is a #1 Amazon bestselling author of sexy, heartfelt contemporary romance and romantic comedies. She writes sassy, quirky heroines, swoony heroes who love their women hard, panty-melting sexytimes, romantic happily ever afters, and all the big feels.

She can't imagine life without coffee, her Kindle, and the sexy heroes who inhabit her imagination. She lives in the inland Pacific Northwest with her three kids.

www.clairekingsleybooks.com

Made in United States
Orlando, FL
14 January 2024